"My hero!"

Juliana's voice rang with adoration.

"I would rather live out our Gothic novel in a hovel with you, than be a princess in a castle. I want only you," she assured him. "Never change, my love."

He hugged her close. "By God, no. I shall always be the man I am now."

"Then I ask no more. To—to the devil with that odious starched-up Lord Ranceford."

He gave her an enigmatic glance. "You are quite sure I'll make a satisfactory substitute?"

Raising her face, she smiled at him fondly. "I'll accept no substitute for you."

He kissed the tip of her nose. "In that case, I'll see you at your wedding."

"You won't fail me, will you?" she asked for good measure.

"I'll be there, I swear it," he told her. "And I promise you shall not marry against your will."

Books by Winifred Witton

HARLEQUIN REGENCY ROMANCE
46–LADY ELMIRA'S EMERALD
54–THE DENVILLE DIAMOND

THE MASKED MARQUIS

WINIFRED WITTON

Harlequin Books

TORONTO • NEW YORK • LONDON
AMSTERDAM • PARIS • SYDNEY • HAMBURG
STOCKHOLM • ATHENS • TOKYO • MILAN
MADRID • WARSAW • BUDAPEST • AUCKLAND

For Dorsey, Maralys, June,
Barbara and Vickie

"Let other pens dwell on guilt and misery. I quit
such odious subjects..."

Jane Austen
Mansfield Park, 1814

Published May 1992

ISBN 0-373-31174-5

THE MASKED MARQUIS

CHAPTER ONE

THE SECOND VOLUME of the latest Gothic novel from Hookam's Lending Library flew from behind the faded curtains hiding the window-seat and landed, pages bent, on the bedchamber floor.

"Maudlin fustian!" Disgusted, Miss Juliana Beveridge gave her cropped blond curls a shake and tucked her feet beneath her on the bench. Real life was nothing like an idiotish novel. Instead of leaping to the aid of a damsel in distress, gentlemen were far more likely to calculate first the amount of her dowry. The age of chivalry was long gone, replaced by the power of pence, pounds, and prestige, none of which could be associated with the House of Beveridge.

She could not blame poor Papa. Gaming was in his blood. Generations of luckless Beveridge baronets had reduced the family to near penury, and Juliana herself to a down-to-earth damsel scornful of romantic dreams—and particularly scornful of Gothic heroines. Surely, in this enlightened year of 1815, a female ought to show some spirit, even when flattened between marbled covers.

Adorinda, the most tiresome heroine yet, had just fainted for the fifth time in as many chapters, merely because she'd been abducted by the evil Count Valnescue, imprisoned in a tower, rescued from seduction in the nick of time by her noble lover, Lord Eduardo, and chastely kissed by her hero. And the bird-witted female had not even kissed him back! Her beloved Eduardo would eventually doom the dastardly villain to a horrible demise and save his constantly fainting Adorinda—though why he wanted a hen-witted female in such poor health was quite beyond Juliana—but he would certainly not do so until the end of Volume Three, and Juliana, if not Adorinda, would before that time have lost all patience.

But that was no excuse to damage the book wilfully. She directed a guilty frown at the crumpled pages. To see a book so mishandled went against the grain. Swinging her feet down to the floor, she smoothed the skirt of her faded sprig muslin morning gown and picked up the despised novel, carefully straightening the creased pages.

"I do beg your pardon," she told them. It was, after all, not their fault they had been cursed with an overly sentimental authoress. As she stood with the book in her hands, her father looked in at her open door.

"Hallo, puss." Sir Agramont Beveridge ambled in, resplendent, if one did not look too closely, in a wine velvet dressing-gown with a matching puckered cap on his balding pate. "Reading, eh?" He meandered over to the mantel and absently rearranged the three chipped figurines and a pair of tarnished candelabra.

"The most ridiculous tale," she told him, tossing the rejected volume onto her dressing-table. She replaced the objects on the mantel with care, exactly where they'd been. "Such things do not happen in this modern age. A man could not force a lady to wed him by imprisoning her in a tower, and surely that ridiculous Lord Eduardo had only to call in the Bow Street Runners and come right up to Count Valnescue's door and demand her release."

She paused, for Sir Agramont's manner seemed odd. Shifting nervously from foot to foot, he let his eyes wander about the room, looking everywhere but at her face. Then he wiped a drop of perspiration from his upper lip and she noticed the frayed edges of his cuffs. Could she turn them for him yet again? Her suspicious gaze softened.

"What is it now, Papa?"

"Nothing. Nothing. That is—" He glanced at her quickly and hastened into speech. "I have only now had another formal visit from Percy. He has come to offer for you again."

Percival Woffington Netherfield was a distant cousin and her father's heir, not that Sir Agramont Beveridge, who was always in dun territory, had anything to leave but his title. Juliana considered Percy an overweight, effeminate rattle with only one redeeming quality. He was wealthy, and that, in her father's eyes, made him an ideal *parti* for his only child. Juliana's features were quite well enough, though she might not be considered an accredited beauty. Her

eyes were blue, her smile a delight, her curls golden—
and her pockets to let. Suitors were not beating a path
to the door of Beveridge House.

Not that she was too concerned. Juliana had no use
for the fops and dandies one met at balls, and even less
for punctilious, high-in-the-instep fashionables interested only in their own consequence. Currently she
was courted only by Percy, and Juliana was uncomfortably aware that she was her father's hedge against
Fleet Street. His creditors held off only because they
expected her to make this advantageous marriage. But
she could not!

"What, commit myself for life to such a mutton-
headed fribble? Never!"

"Are you sure you could not see your way—?"

"No!"

Sir Agramont shuffled his feet and stole a glance
sideways at her adamant expression. "It would solve
all our problems, my love. Perhaps you could think
about it," he added with the hopeful look of a dog
eyeing a table scrap. "Percy is excellent ton. A dependable sort of man. And he offers a substantial settlement."

"Which you would gamble away before the year is
out. No, Papa, I will not be sold like a prize heifer to
supply you with pin money." She regretted the words
as soon as they were out, and hastened to give him an
apologetic hug.

He patted her cheek. "Well, now, puss, since you
put it that way, I cannot but agree with you. In fact,

you are perfectly right. We need a fortune far greater than Percy's. Tell you what, I'll look round. Don't trouble that pretty head about me. I shall come about.''

Her father was serious. Juliana studied him, unable to catch his eye, and grew uneasy. ''Your debts have never bothered you before.''

''Nor do they now.'' He shook off his worried air, and produced a square card from a capacious pocket. ''Here, my girl, see what has come,'' he announced, bright with false cheer. ''An invitation to your god-mama's masquerade.''

Dear Lady Robertshaw! A bosom bow of Juliana's late mother, she always included her goddaughter in her parties, providing the girl with her only social life. And a masquerade!

That meant a costume. Juliana's pleasure dimmed. What could she wear? Amelia Robertshaw's ball-room would be filled with Queen Elizabeths and Madame Pompadours. She could not go as a shepherdess again. Nor would she attend as the fainting Ador-inda, whose pure white gown never showed a trace of the mud and brambles through which both the evil count and the noble Lord Eduardo continually dragged her.

Sir Agramont, seeing her apparently absorbed in happy thought, sidled from the room. As she watched him leave, Juliana had an inspiration.

She pulled the bell rope by her door. As usual, nothing happened. Beveridge House, though still maintaining a respectable front, was not overburdened with servants. Even Conkley, her father's valet, deigned to serve as butler on the rare occasions when they entertained a guest. Mrs. Conkley, their cook, also did the housekeeping, aided by two underhousemaids in training for more profitable positions elsewhere.

Juliana went in search of her abigail, a niece of the Conkleys who had been with her for three years, ever since Juliana left the schoolroom at age fifteen. Emily Jane was a raw country girl willing to accept short wages in return for a chance to see London Town. Unfortunately, for she was a girl of spirit, she was kept rigorously in line by her formidable aunt.

Juliana located her in the kitchen sipping a dish of tea with Mrs. Conkley. Emily Jane sprang to her feet when she saw her mistress and Juliana hastily rescued the cup. With a benign smile, the cook righted the teapot.

"Conky," Juliana began at once. "I need Emily Jane to help me formulate a costume. My godmama, Lady Robertshaw, has invited me to a masquerade."

Emily Jane squealed, awestruck, and Mrs. Conkley flapped her apron at her.

"Ooh," Emily Jane exclaimed, unabashed. "You'll 'ave to wear a mask! And dance w' mysterious gentlemen, all romantic and such!"

"As for that," said Mrs. Conkley repressively, "our lady will 'ave no truck with them as she don't know. I'll warrant Mr. Percy will be there. We'll dress you up pretty as a picture, Miss Julie, and then see if he don't offer for you on the spot.''

"He has offered, Conky, and I don't want him.'' With an impatient gesture, Juliana brushed Percy aside like the annoying insect she thought him. "I'll be no simpering Gothic maiden looking for romance. But I haven't the jewels to wear as a great lady, nor have I the wherewithal to rent a gorgeous costume. My rig must be something that we have already at hand, and I have had a splendid idea. I shall go as Portia, a no-nonsense character I have always admired.''

The Conkleys, aunt and niece, looked blank.

"A heroine from Shakespeare,'' Juliana explained. "In *The Merchant of Venice*. She wears a robe when she disguises herself as a lawyer, and I have thought of my father's wine velvet dressing-gown. There is a great deal of material and it can easily be altered. Mayhap it can even be reconstructed afterwards, should he want it back. The sleeves must be shortened anyway,'' she added, "so really it will be doing him a favour, and it will be the very thing for a lady of solemn mien. We can dress my hair high beneath the matching cap, which really looks rather Elizabethan already, and I shall carry a book.''

Mrs. Conkley stared at her, aghast. "You'll never go as a bluestocking! Turn off every man who sees you, you will! Pretty miss like you, ducks. Be a real shame, it would, if Mr. Percy finds you're bookish.''

A line from *The Merchant* popped into Juliana's head and she recited it with an impish grin. "I 'fish

not, with . . . this melancholy bait,' and certainly not
'for this fool's gudgeon.' Come, Emily Jane, we go to
divest my father of his velvet garb.''

Emily Jane squealed again, shocked and thrilled at
so outrageous a suggestion. Juliana caught her hand
and dragged her from the kitchen.

ON THE MORE fashionable side of Town, another invitation to the Robertshaws' masquerade waited on an
inlaid Italian table in the hall of an elegant mansion.
In the bookroom, seated by the hearth, the Marquis
of Ranceford's thoughts were not on masquerades—
as yet. In his lap lay a copy of *The Corsair*, fresh from
the pen of George Gordon, Lord Byron, which he had
been reading "again, again—and oft again."

He looked down at his long legs, encased in skin-
tight fawn inexpressibles, at his gleaming Hessians,
polished with French champagne, one ankle now
negligently crossed over the other. His coat of blue
superfine—from the hands of Weston, of course—
clung to shoulders which needed no wadding to increase their breadth. His mirror told him the clean-cut
features above his beautifully creased Oriental were
handsome, extremely so, and a lock of his carefully
tousselled dark hair hung romantically over his forehead. There were no two ways about it. He was perfect.

Ranceford uncrossed his impeccably shod ankles
and recrossed them the other way. Wasted, all wasted,
in these dreary modern days when manners and fash-

ion were all. No scope in London for a Corsair. And no water near, save the Thames. It would be hard to be a pirate in a skulling boat. But what a Corsair he could have been! Instead, he was trapped in a prison without bars, managing a large estate and raising his late brother's numerous offspring.

I'm nearing thirty, he thought, *and have never done anything exciting or dangerous.* Napoleon had caused him to miss the Grand Tour, and being head of his family, he couldn't go to the War. He had never *meant* to be the Marquis of Ranceford, believing that position securely held by his older brother. David, however, had inconsiderately killed himself five years before while attempting a regular rasper on the hunting field, leaving only daughters and not a single son.

Rance picked up *The Corsair* and read again Byron's description of Conrad the Corsair. "Fire in his glance, and wildness in his breast . . . the distant mien that . . . awes if seen." There was a *man,* pursuing the dreams of every shackled male. Ah, to "snatch the life of Life," as Conrad did. Rance sighed for what could never be.

The reason for his frustration, his widowed sister-in-law, chose that moment to burst into his private domain with a swirl of skirts and a blast of cheer. He dropped his book hastily, annoyed to find himself feeling guilty.

"The most delightful thing, Ranceford!" Lady Clara started in at once, her stylishly cropped and tinted curls bobbing in excitement. Though on the shady side of forty, she maintained an annoyingly youthful outlook. She had once had a pretty face, but Rance now thought it sadly disfigured by her constantly open mouth. She rattled on happily. "I have been visiting dearest Lady Catherine Moffet this past half hour. She has received an invitation to attend a young people's masquerade at the Robertshaws' so of course I hurried home at once and yes, here is yours, come while I was away."

Rance, who had risen politely, sank back into his chair. Masquerades were not his idea of delight.

Clara babbled on, neither expecting an answer nor turning an ear should he make one. "You must give a masquerade for our Augusta after her come-out next year. A costume affair is of all things the ideal way to present a young lady at her most romantic—and one for Rosamund, and Ophelia, and..."

Her words did not cease. Rance simply stopped listening. There were five of those confounded girls. He faced a devilish future. Five come-out balls, five routs, soirées, drums, Venetian breakfasts, al fresco parties and more parties. Rance shuddered. And he'd be expected to host them all. Suddenly Clara's words broke through his protective barrier.

"Henry VIII," she was saying. "I've already sent James—or was it Robert? Whatever, one of them—to the costumier in King Street to reserve your costume."

"Clara, I have no intention of making a cake of myself in hose and bloomers. If I go, I'll wear a respectable domino."

She rolled over him like an avalanche. "Of course, you will be Henry. Lady Catherine will expect it. She purposely told me she was planning to be Catherine Howard, Henry's fifth wife—or was it Catherine of Aragon, his first—or perhaps Catherine Parr, who was the sixth? He married so many Catherines. I am quite sure it was one of them. It matters not a jot, you may be the same Henry for all. When she told me whom she was to be, I knew at once she wished you to be her Henry. Why do you not offer for her, Ranceford? I am sure she has been attempting to bring you up to scratch this past year or more, and you could not find a more suitable match. A most excellent Catherine for your Henry."

"She wishes me to have her beheaded?" he asked, mildly hopeful.

"Do not be frivolous, Ranceford. It is not fitting for a man in your position. I do hope that marriage with such a well-bred female as Lady Catherine will give your mind a more serious turn. You will need a wig." She spun on her heel and made for the door. "I declare, I believe I forgot to tell Robert—or James, whichever—to be sure to ask for one, and for extra padding for the front. If it is Catherine Parr, Henry was quite corpulent by then."

Rance ceased arguing, not that Clara had given him a chance. She was out of the room before any words could leave his mouth. He watched her brisk departure with "the fetter'd captive's mourning eye That weeps for flight." He sighed again, and picking up *The Corsair,* sought solace. It was easier to give in to Clara, who would keep on and on about any subject once it became fixed in what he loosely termed her mind. After all, what did it matter? It would be a dull party, one of hundreds in his dull future.

But he would not offer for the dull Catherine Moffet. It was incumbent on him to eventually marry and produce an heir, but there were other women, even in *The Corsair.* Conrad's fair Medora utterly failed to capture his romantic dreams. As a bride who could not even stay alive to welcome home her hero, she left much to be desired. Conrad should have stayed with his Gulnare. Rance himself had no intention of being saddled with Lady Catherine, a Medora if he'd ever seen one, though there was not much chance of Catherine dying young. She seemed remarkably healthy.

But not as healthy as he had thought. Barely two days had passed when Lady Clara broke in on him again with a tragic face.

"A message by hand, Ranceford," she exclaimed, waving a sheet of writing paper. "She is dreadfully sorry."

Rance, once more absorbed in dreaming over *The Corsair,* raised vague eyes. "Who is sorry?"

"Why, Lady Catherine, of course. But she must be forgiven. She has sent a most apologetic note."

Intrigued, Rance closed the book, marking the place with one finger. "Why? Whatever has she done?"

"Oh, it is not she. It is young Hubert."

"Ah, has he broken one of our windows again?" Catherine's eight-year-old sibling was like to do this when playing at ball. That, or fight with one of Clara's extensive brood and smash beds of new tulips.

Clara waxed indignant. "No such thing! The poor little angel has come down with an infectious complaint and she cannot come to dine with us tonight for she must stay at his side. He weeps if she leaves."

Ranceford saw no reason for tears of his own. "Send our condolences," he said cheerfully. "No doubt all will come right soon." And he could now have a pleasant dinner at one of his clubs instead.

"This is dreadful!" Clara exclaimed, having referred to the message again. "They are to take Hubert to the country for a month, on a repairing lease. Ranceford! She will be unable to attend the Robertshaws' masquerade. This is of all things the most inconvenient. I have already ordered for you a magnificent regalia from the costumier."

"Then you may cancel it," said Rance, greatly relieved. "I shan't have to go."

"Not go! Certainly you will go. Amelia Robertshaw is one of my dearest friends."

"Then *you* go."

"What? And have to listen to a rodomontade on all her imagined ills? I cannot abide the woman for longer than a half-hour visit."

"Splendid. We shall both remain at home."

Clara shook her head firmly. "You *must* go. I have given my word that not only will you be present, but you will be seen to stand up twice with each of her girls. It is such a cachet for them to be escorted by a marquis. You will be able to do so with ease now that you need not be dancing attendance on Catherine. I had meant to go as her chaperon, but now I have no reason and an excellent excuse. Ethelinda has the earache—the roasted onion poultice has done no good whatsoever—and unless I am vastly mistaken, Mirabella is coming down with the measles, for I have heard of several cases among their friends."

She stopped speaking, a speculative gleam in her protuberant eyes. "I daresay I know what has happened." She tapped the stiff edge of Catherine's note against her large front teeth. "She seemed a trifle out of frame when I called on her last week. Not at all in plump currant. I'll wager it is she and not Hubert who must retire to the country. I shall go at once to pen her a sympathetic word, hoping for a speedy recovery."

Ranceford remained where he was, a fantastic thought having struck him. Napoleon was defeated, duelling illegal, Mohocks no longer prowled the streets, and the only place a man could wear a sword was at a masquerade.

And he could handle that sword. Several hours a week, he practiced with the best fencing master in London, but to no avail. He'd never meet his man to the tune of ringing steel on steel in the grey misty dawn at Paddington Fields, or save a damsel from the Fate Worse Than Death with his brilliant swordplay as he pursued a dastardly villain through an ogre-ridden castle on a moor. He'd been born a hundred years too late. One could hardly swashbuckle, even at a masquerade, when escorting a lady like Catherine, but now... Suppose instead of King Henry, he became— for one night!—Conrad the Corsair?

The idea took hold. Why not? Why go as a six-teenth-century courtier or in a simple domino, both considered the only garb appropriate for a man in his position? He would be masked, after all. Why not go as the man he longed to be? No long curls, plumed hats and velvet doublets. Like the Corsair, he felt "the exulting sense—the pulse's maddening play, That thrills...and turns what some deem danger to delight." Lord Byron knew whereof he spoke. In such a dis-guise, he might even meet a Gulnare without Lady Catherine's disapproving presence. Although, he ad-mitted, that was too much for which to hope. Gul-nare's costume was hardly one a lady of the ton would wear, if the paintings of Delacroix and Gericault were to be believed.

In fact, he was not at all sure what a Corsair would wear, not being accustomed to moving in the same circles as a pirate. Indeed, he gave a wide berth to ships and the sea, for he became deplorably seasick when-ever he crossed the Channel.

He could see himself dressed all in black from head to toe: a black cape lined with red silk, a black beaver hat, and a mask—a strip of black silk with eyeholes large enough not to impair his vision. And then, of course, there was the sword. A rapier perhaps, although a cutlass would be best, except that it would be heavy and hard to manage while dancing a quadrille. He decided to settle for his fencing foil with the button removed.

Oh, but he'd make all the other gentlemen look dandified and effeminate in their wigs and satins! And he wouldn't be unmasked. Maybe he'd even kiss as many of the ladies in the moonlight as he could manage, and instead of dancing, he'd stride across the ballroom brushing men aside—only his friends, of course: it wouldn't do to precipitate an illegal duel with some stranger. Besides, Clara would never allow it. Oh, devil take it, he knew he'd do no such thing. Daydreaming was a dangerous pastime for one unused to such heady pleasures.

But be the Corsair for that one night, he would.

Rance laid his plans with care, considering every contingency, for it would never do for this scheme to reach the ears of Lady Clara. No dreams could withstand the blazing light of a scoffing woman, and scoffing from the materialistic Clara was a certainty. As far as she was concerned, Henry VIII must remain on his throne.

To this end, Rance sought out a base for his activities during the next two weeks. It had to be somewhere he was not known. He settled finally on a rather obscure tavern called The Coach and Horses, on

Nightingale Street in East Smithfield, a place he was assured no questions were asked and no answers given. He hired a private room in which to don his costume, the only one in the inn, and paid in advance for two weeks' lodging and stabling for a horse.

He had to have a horse. No self-respecting Corsair would travel on land in so plebian a conveyance as a modern curricle. And no animal from his own stable would do, for his cattle were well known. Besides, he needed a solid black without betraying markings. The more he imagined his Corsair, the more romantic the colour black became, and the more the mystery aspect appealed.

He could not go to Tattersall's, where he was far better known than his horses. He had taken to roaming about Smithfield to familiarize himself with the streets in the darkness of night, and it was at a country fair that he finally located a proper Corsair's steed. He soon found why it was for sale. A fiery, coal-black gelding, it proved to be a fractious mount. Flighty and headstrong, it was useless for hunting, unpleasant in all its gaits, and no good for park hacking. In short, a flashy beast, quite in order for his romantic rider.

His costume proved as much trouble as the horse. When questioned, the costumier in King Street had definite ideas about the proper garb for a pirate, none of which agreed with Rance's mental image. The man did, however, produce a beautiful crimson-lined black cloak that was exactly right, and a wide-brimmed Spanish hat which, once the colourful trimming was removed, proved really quite dashing. Rance also purchased a seventeenth-century belt and scabbard for his unbuttoned foil. He sacrificed a good black silk neckcloth, cutting eyeholes and narrowing it to cover only the upper part of his face. He carried his purchases secretly up to his chambers, put them all on and gazed into his dressing-table glass. His heart skipped a beat as Conrad the Corsair, just as he'd imagined him, gazed back. The masked marquis was ready.

And none too soon. The great night had arrived.

In the interest of peace in the home, it was expedient not to arouse the curiosity of Lady Clara. Henry VIII drove his curricle sedately to East Smithfield, where Rance stabled his equipage. He changed costumes in his private room and saddled the black gelding, not without some difficulty. The horse snorted and danced until Rance realized his flapping cloak caused the air-brained beast to panic. It was some time before the two came to terms, much to the entertainment of a few stable-boys, but at last the Corsair rode off.

His spirits soared as his mount crow-hopped and shied along the road towards Hounslow Heath, and Rance regretted that the Bow Street Horse Patrol, operating there since 1805, had rid the area of highwaymen. He was quite in the mood for a confrontation and, even though he felt a trifle foolish, he couldn't resist tying on his mask, loosening the foil in its scabbard, and entering into his part.

Then, halfway to the Robertshaws' country estate, he heard a single shot from beyond a copse at a bend in the road.

It was followed by a shrill, feminine scream.

CHAPTER TWO

JULIANA LET DOWN the window of her unfashionable carriage and peered out into the moonlit road. "Do hush, Emily Jane," she said. "It is only a single footpad barring our way."

The abigail, already out of her forward seat, crowded up behind her. "Lawks, Miss Julie," she exclaimed. "I ain't afeared. Seemed like one o' us shoulda let out a 'oller, so I did." She squinted at the dark figure menacing them with a long-barrelled pistol. "Ooh, 'e's a bad 'un, 'e is!"

"Nonsense, Emily Jane. Actually, he looks rather harmless."

Untangling herself from the heavy folds of the sumptuous Portia costume she and the maid had contrived from Sir Agramont's wine velvet dressing-gown, Juliana clambered down. Emily Jane came close behind. The elderly coachman already stood in the road, the ancient musket which lived under his seat on the ground before him.

Juliana, imbued with the dramatic character of Portia, faced the highwayman with bravado. He did not look at all like her idea of a villainous bandit. A weedy little man, no taller than herself, he wore a slouch hat and a dirty muffler wrapped about the lower part of his face. Tattered herdsman's boots, consisting of strips of old blanketing tied in place with spirals of leather, covered what she could see of his legs below an ancient frieze coat several sizes too big for him. Even his pistol was too large for his hands.

"Let us pass," she commanded imperiously.

"Not till I 'ave yer—yer valables." The pistol, aimed now at her, trembled in his grasp. "Give 'em over."

Juliana/Portia drew herself up. "I will do no such thing."

"Yus, yer will. This 'ere's a real robbery."

She stamped her foot. "Pick up your gun, John," she demanded of her driver. "Shoot him."

John Coachman leaned towards her and hissed in her ear, keeping one eye on their captor. "Can't, Miss Julie. I don't keep no powder in that there musket. That'ud be right dangerous."

The road agent apparently felt it was time he rejoined the conversation. He waved the long-barrelled pistol. "'And over yer jewels," he ordered loudly.

"I don't have any," Juliana told him. "Thankfully, this costume did not require them."

As she spoke, hoofbeats pounded on the hard road and a startling apparition dashed round the bend, a man mounted on a black horse and dressed all in black. A crimson-lined cape swirled behind him and a silken loo-type mask concealed his upper features. He leapt from his rearing, dancing steed and tied his reins to a tree branch, rather more securely than Juliana thought necessary. While she stared in amazement, he drew a slender sword and advanced on the highwayman, taking a fencing stance with one arm high and the foil extended.

"Hold, varlet," he declaimed.

"I be 'olding," said the robber. "'Olding me barker. Put up that frog sticker, cully, or I blow a 'ole clean through yer afore yer can get a whiff o' me."

The masked man, now fairly close, wrinkled his nose. "There you mistake, my good fellow. I daresay you can't remember when last you bathed."

Deeply offended, the highwayman turned the pistol on him and took aim.

"Portia's" sense of justice was outraged. So unequal a confrontation would not do! The man holding the pistol now had his back to her. Juliana caught up John Coachman's heavy musket, swung it high above her head and with all her strength, brought the solid wooden stock down on the hapless robber's skull. He dropped like a felled ox.

The masked man, taken aback, lowered his sword.

"Remove his pistol, sir," Juliana commanded him in her best Portia manner. "If the poor creature will but take this as an admirable lesson and tread the straight and narrow path from this day forward, he will have no need of a firearm."

"Coo," Emily Jane remarked from the safety of her position behind John Coachman. "'Ave you killed 'im, Miss Julie?"

"I certainly hope not." Juliana had had the same unpleasant thought. It occurred to her that it might be improvident not to exit the scene, and she "stood not upon the order of her going." Pushing the unwilling abigail back into the carriage, she climbed in after her, and called the coachman out of his catatonic state. "Drive on, John, at once!"

As the coach lumbered away, Juliana leaned back against the worn squabs, ignoring Emily Jane's excited chatter. She felt quite smug. She had had her chance to act a damsel in distress like a simpering Gothic heroine and be saved by that lovely masked man with his cape and sword. But did she faint like the missish Adorinda? She did not. *She* saved *him*. She giggled. It must have annoyed the poor man terribly, quite ruining his rescue. But then he shouldn't have acted the romantic idiot and challenged a man holding a pistol when he himself wielded only a sword. What could she have done but grab John Coachman's musket and strike down the villain before he could shoot? What a shame it would have been if a common footpad had slain so gallant a swashbuckler! Really, the masked man was most intriguing.

She knew a flicker of surprise. Intriguing? A silly, melodramatic, Gothic hero?

RANCEFORD FELT VERY SILLY indeed. How could one rescue a maiden who took the matter right out of one's hands? And of all the overbearing creatures he'd ever met! Ordering him about as if she were the Queen of

England! He left the gun where it lay, a useless gesture which didn't make him feel a bit better.

The fallen highwayman was another matter.

He sprawled in a pathetic heap in the roadway, blood dribbling from a gash in his head. Rance frowned down at him. What the devil was he to do? He couldn't leave the confounded fellow lying there with a split skull. Making a pad of his handkerchief, he knelt and stanched the blood, finding that the damnably efficient female's victim had apparently sustained no permanent damage. Scalps always bled horrifically.

Nothing the little thief wore was fit to use as a bandage. Regretfully, Rance sacrificed his own new black neckcloth and bound the pad in place. But now what would he do? The blasted woman had placed him in an impossible position. He was on horseback. If he'd kept to his curricle, he could have transported the unconscious man to the nearest inn and left him in the charge of the barkeep for a few pounds. He could hardly count on that goose-rumped black bone-rattler to carry double. If only the bloody corpse would wake up...

As if in answer, the injured man stirred and opened one eye. He groaned and looked up at Rance. "Go on," he said in a weak voice. "Why don'tcher kill me the rest o' the way?"

"Why?" It seemed to Rance an unusual request.

"I'm fer the nubbin' cheat out Tyburn way any means, and I druther be stabbed w' that there sword."

Ranceford picked up the man's antique flintlock, examining it with interest. "Wouldn't you prefer me to shoot you instead?"

"Yer can't. That there pistol ain't been reloaded. Only 'ad the blunt fer one ball." The highwayman tried to sit up. "Devil take me," he moaned, clutching his temples and screwing his eyes shut. "Wot 'it me?"

Rance's lips tightened. "The lady," he said shortly.

He felt shrewd eyes appraising what could be seen of him in the moonlight. The little highwayman came to a decision.

"Owin' to yer interference, cocky, I ain't got the rhino to pay me shot at the tavern. I s'pose yer couldn't see yer way to standin' fer a kip and doss-down till I gets me 'ead workin' agin?"

Ranceford sighed, knowing the man had read him correctly. He fished his card case from a pocket, extracted one, and scribbled a note on the back.

"Go to this address. My man will see that you get some decent clothes and a meal. Ask for Mr. Beasley." He handed the card over, along with half a crown.

The highwayman gasped and staggered to his feet. Rance steadied him for a minute until he got his balance. The wiry little thief barely came to his shoulder.

"I 'ave ter thank yer, me friend."

"Forget it."

"That I won't, cully. Yer done me a good deed and I never fergets a favour. Should yer ever need a 'elpin 'and, call fer One-eye Willyum at the Nag's Head in Covent Garden, corner o' James and Floral Streets, back o' the Oprey 'Ouse.''

Rance bent down to give him a closer look. "Yes, I thought so. You have two eyes."

"Aye, but Two-eye Willyum ain't so pichurskew a 'andle."

The marquis noticed suddenly that the black horse had begun to rear back, attempting to pull down the tree he had tied him to. "Hop it," he told the highwayman, and started for his troublesome mount. By the time he had fought his way into the saddle, the man had disappeared into the night.

The Marquis of Ranceford, not Conrad the Corsair, proceeded on his way to the masquerade, hampered by his erratic mount and thoroughly annoyed by the fiasco his first adventure had become. Why was it so infernally difficult to be a swashbuckling hero? Ordinary men used to do it all the time. Surely all damsels in distress would not be so confoundedly self-reliant as this last one. He was perfect for a Corsair. What had gone wrong?

Still in somewhat of a dudgeon, he entered the Robertshaws' front hall and paused by a wall mirror to adjust his neckcloth. Only then did he remember that he'd last seen it wrapped about the no doubt vermin-ridden head of One-eye Willyum.

But a man of his consequence couldn't appear in public in a state of undress! He studied his reflection again. The open shirt collar gave him a dashing look, far more buccaneerish than the staid neckcloth in his familiar Oriental style. He looked a proper pirate! Feeling inordinately pleased with his new image, he adjusted his mask and tilted the wide-brimmed Spanish hat at a more jaunty angle. Were it not for the hidebound tenets of the ton and the sartorial heritage of Beau Brummel, he might cut quite a swath among his associates with this new style.

He stepped into the ballroom with confidence, and a figure across the floor caught his eye. A regal figure. Her elegant wine velvet robe stood out dramatically among the throng of fussily embellished Queen Elizabeths and Madame Pompadours.

Good God, if she saw him and recounted the earlier event of the evening to her friends, he would be a laughing-stock!

He pressed through the crowd, over to an open French window, and slipped out onto the terrace. He was leaning over the low wall, trying to determine the quickest way across the grounds to the stable where he'd left that damnable horse, when a footstep sounded behind him. Someone else had come out that open window. He turned... Oh, blast! It was that dratted female, and she had seen him.

She stopped, startled, one hand at her breast. "You!" she exclaimed. "You have followed me!"

Rance gave a resigned shrug. What could he do but play his part until he could escape? He swept a low, and he hoped romantically Corsairish, bow.

"What man could resist such a challenge?" His voice when he spoke was low and throbbing. Low because he didn't want to be heard by anyone inside that window, and throbbing because his throat had grown excessively tight with raw nerves. Suppose, having had this second look at him, she would recognize him if they met later?

Juliana, in spite of her dislike of foolish melodrama, was conscious of a tingling thrill. "You should not have followed me." She had a sudden horrid thought. "Do not say you have come to tell me I killed that bandit!"

The masked man hastened to reassure her, as though he feared she might be about to faint. "No, no such thing. A mere scalp wound. I bound up his head and sent him on his way."

"Sir, how can I thank you?" She felt the colour return to her cheeks. "But suppose you are discovered here? You must not stay!"

He apparently had no intention of doing so. His hands were already on the low wall, ready to vault over but, indeed, the scene seemed to call for another line. He bowed again. "Fair maiden, I would risk my life for a moment of your company."

Juliana giggled. "I cannot claim it is worth such a sacrifice." Truly, the masked man played a most amusing game, and she was quite ready to enter into the spirit. Why not? Obviously, he was a gentleman. There was little enough fun in her life, and this silly would-be hero was tall and broad-shouldered. What little she could see of his face, really only his quirking smile, was pleasing. She dropped him a curtsy. "You make me a very pretty compliment, Sir Masquerader."

To her delight, he seized his cue. "But set me a quest, my lady, for I am yours to command. I live only to rescue damsels in distress. I shall do better next time," he added, provoking her into a laugh.

"Who are you, sir?" she asked. "How may I reach you, should I need to be rescued once more?"

For a moment he seemed stumped, and then visited by inspiration. "You have but to leave a message at the Nag's Head Inn in Covent Garden for One-eye Will-yum."

She gasped. "Is *that* your name?"

He sounded as repulsed at the idea as she. "Good God, no, but he can find me. I beg you," he added anxiously, "do not go there yourself. It is not a place for ladies."

"Indeed, I shall not," she assured him. "I recall seeing the sign once—a circus horse, is it not?—when I attended the Royal Opera House and the carriage approached Covent Garden by way of James Street. It looked a very low tavern." She considered him, curious. What acquaintance could so gentlemanly a masked man have in so disreputable an inn? "Is this One-eye Willyum a friend of yours?"

"Certainly not! As a matter of fact, he is the man you struck down. In turn for not spitting him on my sword as he requested, he offered to do me a favour, and I can think of nothing I'd like more than a chance to redeem myself in your eyes. Do, I beg of you—"

"Wait! Tell me at once. Why did he wish you to spit him upon your sword? I must know."

"Why, because he had not another ball for his pistol."

Juliana nodded wisely. "Of course. I quite see. And this suicidal, er, person will contact you from the next world, if need be?"

The generous mouth beneath the black mask widened into a grin. "Promise me you will send him notice immediately should you require another rescue. I shall take pains to inform him that he should not be its cause."

"For that, I thank you." For some reason, Juliana wanted to prolong this interview. Never before had she spoken so freely to an engaging man, feeling no need to be on her manners lest he find some excuse to leave her side to pursue a more eligible young lady. A romantic, play-acting coxcomb he might be, but for the moment at least, he was *her* coxcomb. She dropped him another curtsy.

"Have you not another name?" she asked. "One by which I may know you?"

Rance hesitated, and came to a decision. "Conrad," he said. "Pray call me Conrad."

"Conrad! Are you then pretending to be that ridiculous Corsair?"

"Ridiculous!"

"Of all the idiotish men! To return to his insipid Medora when he could have stayed with the enterprising Gulnare. There he had found a female who acted upon her principles, and he left her!"

This so closely agreed with his own opinion that Rance shut the mouth he had opened to defend his hero.

"It is my belief," the girl went on, "that Lord Byron did not finish his great opus as he should have. Had I been the author, Conrad would have buried his passive bride, rejoined Gulnare, who was worth two of Medora, and then sailed away with her across the sea. I should not have written him as such a nodcock."

Rance frowned. This was not at all the attitude he expected a female to take. She should be admiring his hero—and, therefore, himself—not belittling Byron's melodramatic tale. How much easier for a poet to write a scene than for a human actor to attempt the role when the heroine did not speak the proper lines!

The girl was studying what she could see of his features. "Sir, will you not take off your mask here where we are private?"

He shook his head. After what she had said about idiotic nodcocks? "Never!"

She nodded again. "You are very right, sir. It would not do to destroy the mystery. I am quite tempted to carry on our game, but you had best leave. Only think if you should be discovered by our host!"

Rance barely stopped himself before telling her not to fear, that he was an invited guest. Indeed, he was well-known to the Robertshaws, but he had no intention of being caught out in his present guise.

The girl stepped closer. "I almost feel I know you, sir. Why will you not unmask?"

"You gave answer yourself, fair lady," he replied, thinking fast. "It would make an end to our diverting fantasy." And an end to him if that dreadful girl discovered his identity and spread this evening's embarrassing doings abroad. He would never live it down! To be saved from a bandit half his size, and who possessed only an unloaded pistol, by a slip of a girl who knocked the robber unconscious with a single blow! What a figure of fun he'd appear to all his acquaintance.

The only thing to do was make this interlude one she'd not care to divulge. And that called for a daring deed he'd never have contemplated in his true character. Acting the swashbuckling Corsair, he swept the startled girl into his arms for a long and passionate kiss.

For a few glorious moments he quite forgot himself, as her yielding form melted against him. The fragrance of the roses in her hair, heady as champagne, intoxicated his senses as he nuzzled the satin of her cheek and found the softness of her lips. He felt her tremble. His arms tightened and he deepened the kiss.

Then, as though awakened to reality by her shocking response, she tore herself away, shoving hard at his broad chest.

The low terrace wall was just behind his knees, and below it was a mud-bottomed ornamental pond.

CHAPTER THREE

THE MARQUIS OF RANCEFORD sat in a foot of green water, covered by mire and surrounded by lily pads and startled fancy fish. He picked a vile-smelling strand of pond grass from his cape and attempted to collect his scattered wits.

Amazingly, it was the young lady's response to his sudden embrace which occupied him first, not his subsequently being dumped unceremoniously into the Robertshaws' ornamental water and soaking his inexpressibles. He'd been told well-bred gentlewomen were cold and passive—why, this one had returned his embrace with more warmth than the most mercenary mistress he'd ever kept! In spite of himself, he chuckled. That was one spirited female, but one he planned to avoid like the plague.

He stood up, dripping fronds of aquatic plants and dislodging a large snail from the seat of his muddied breeches. His sodden Corsair costume clung to him, his hip-high black boots were waterlogged and, he suspected, housing a variety of wriggling pond creatures. Slogging to the edge of the pool, he sat down on the low wall surrounding it and emptied his footwear pensively. Now what? It was unthinkable to appear at home in this condition! He could envision Beasley's face when his master strode into his bedchamber dripping slime and assorted pond crawlers on the Aubusson carpet.

However, all was not lost. Thank goodness, he'd had the foresight to obtain two costumes for this unfortunate affair. Well, perhaps Clara had had a lot to do with it, but in any case he now had only grateful thoughts of the nice, dry—and hitherto unappreciated—Henry VIII outfit left behind in his lodging at the Coach and Horses Tavern. Smithfield was only a few miles away.

Twenty minutes later, after a thorough slosh-off under the stable pump—to the delight of a number of grooms playing at Tip Cat in the yard—he was battling the black horse back down the road towards Town.

He turned into the yard at the inn, shoving his mask into a pocket and shouting to an hostler to relieve him of the aggravating beast. The man stared at him, an unneeded reminder of his wet and filthy appearance.

"Cor," the stable-hand remarked admiringly. "Ain't yer the proper mess now! Reckon yer come a cropper offen that flash nag o' yers into a goodly ditch."

The Marquis of Ranceford turned on him, wrathful at the man's insolence. "Clean my saddle," he snapped. "And be sure it's carefully dried."

"Oh, yus, sir." The man bowed low, pulling his forelock. "Right at once, yer royal 'ighness."

Rance drew himself up—and suddenly remembered his costume. Here, he was not a lord. He was a common man. He felt a twinge of surprise at his reaction to the man's impertinence. He had never been one to look down on his servants—there was no need. They kept their places and he had his, taken for granted. It was rather interesting to see the other side. He drew a large coin from his pocket and tossed it to the man. "See that you do a good job," he said, more mildly. "And rub down this damnable beast."

This time he received the reverence he'd expected.

While he transformed himself in the inn from Conrad the Corsair to the much-married king, his mind dwelt on the unknown lady in wine velvet and her unexpected resourcefulness. Suppose he had escorted Lady Catherine Moffet to the masquerade as Clara desired. What would she have done when faced with a pistol-waving highwayman? He grinned as he adjusted Henry's frontal padding. Catherine would have had a fit of the vapours while One-eye Willyum blasted a hole clear through him. Or the man would have, had he been able to afford another ball for his gun.

He tied the ribands below his knees to keep Henry's hose from sagging. Who was the wine-velvet lady? he wondered—and had a horrifying thought. What if she, too, wondered about his own identity and decided to track him down? He had no misapprehensions regarding her abilities. Would she recognize him if he encountered her in his own character, without his mask? He had to know, or go through life skulking behind furniture whenever he ventured out into Society.

Rance faced his difficulty squarely, believing it best to know the worst at once. The night was yet young; the masquerade ball would go on until three or four in the morning. He could be back at the Robertshaws' within the hour if that devil of a horse cooperated. What was he thinking? Truly, that female had him addle-brained! His curricle was here at the inn. He called down for the hostler to harness his pair, and threw his many-caped driving coat over Henry VIII. Being the Corsair had lost some of its glamour.

JULIANA SLIPPED BACK into the ballroom through the open French window, her cheeks blazing. Her hair, never easy to control, felt all disarrayed, ribands and pins slipping from her headdress. She plucked at her high bodice, trying to fluff out the crushed velvet at her neckline. Oh, drat it all! She had gone out on the terrace to avoid the unwelcome advances of one Henry Pontleby, a man whom she was sure her father would characterize as a nasty piece of work, and only see what she had got into instead! Far worse! Shaken to the core, she hurried across the floor, hoping no one would notice her agitation.

That masked man was no gentleman! For all his cultured speech and romantic notions, he was nothing but a bounder—a cad, a loose fish, a skirter, a—a care-for-nobody! Only witness the way he had taken advantage of a helpless female—the way he had kissed her! A rush of heat enveloped her at the memory. Oh, how he had kissed her! She knew men did so, for she was well-read, but she had never imagined the sensations such a kiss would produce. No wonder Adorinda had fainted! For the first time, she felt a kinship with that weak-brained female.

At the double doors to the ballroom, she paused to pat her tumbled curls into place as best she could before running into the Great Hall. At the back, beyond the huge hearth where a whole ox could be turned on a spit, she remembered seeing the green baize doors which led to the servants' wing. If she could find Godmama Amelia's housekeeper, that worthy would summon Emily Jane for her. On arrival, she had turned her young abigail over to the kindly Mrs. Nash with instructions to find a place where the girl could watch the dancing. But she needed her maid to redo her hair at once!

She could not go past those green baize doors. It simply was not done. Fortunately, the hall bustled with domestics setting up the supper tables in the long drawing-room at the front of the house under the direction of the butler. Juliana caught a passing footman by the sleeve and asked him to send Mrs. Nash after her abigail.

A few minutes later, Emily Jane scurried into the hall and stopped short.

"Coo! What 'appened to yer, Miss Julie? Yer all flushed like and yer 'air is a mess!"

Juliana sighed. "Do try for a bit more decorum, Emily Jane."

"Yus, but—"

"Never mind what happened. Come up with me to the ladies' parlour and put my headdress in order. I—I merely had a slight accident."

She was subjected to a shrewd gaze. "Haccident? More likely a hupsetting hexperience," said Emily Jane, who strove to improve her accent whenever she remembered. Then she, too, had a horrid thought. Her round eyes widened alarmingly and her *H*'s went by the board. "Lawks, Miss Julie, yer never on the run? They 'asn't come fer yer fer killin' that there 'ighwayman?"

"No, no." Juliana pushed her towards the stairs. "He's quite all right. Hardly damaged at all."

Emily Jane halted like a balky mule. "And 'ow do yer know that?"

Juliana felt her face ripen like a sun-kissed tomato. She could never keep anything long from her inquisitive abigail, who was as curious, and quick to investigate, as a cat spotting an unknown movement under a bush. She resigned herself to candour.

"The man in the cape came to reassure me, that is all."

"All, is it?" Emily Jane broke the tissue-thin wall of protocol between them and grinned broadly at her mistress. "Best we fix yer 'air up afore yer seen. Come along, then."

Juliana followed her meekly up the stairs.

When she re-entered the ballroom half an hour later, Henry Pontleby threaded his way purposefully towards her through the crowd. How she disliked the man with his perpetually curled lip, his dark hair styled à la Brutus over a thin patrician nose, his eyes too knowing and his manner entirely too familiar! She looked about in desperation.

Percival Woffington Netherfield stood nearby, and for once she was thankful for his presence. She favoured him with a bright welcoming smile, and his face lit up. He fairly pranced to her side. Unfortunately, he had chosen to garb himself as King Louis XIV, and Juliana wondered, with a touch of pity, how men who were negligible in the lower extremities could see fit to opt for overpowering rigs which showed up their spindle-shanks. But Percy meant well and since she needed him at the moment, he was forgiven. Resorting to *The Merchant of Venice,* she quoted to herself, "God made him, and therefore let him pass for a man."

How much more elegant was simple attire, say all black with only a crimson lining to the cape. She was forced to stifle a giggle. She had heard the splash. How was she to know there was a pond right beneath him? She hoped the masked man's lovely costume was not completely ruined.

Percy reached her side minutes before Pontleby could escape from the crush. He made an elaborate leg, brushing the floor with his hand in a sweeping gesture before kissing her fingertips. Really, she thought critically, the masked man—gentleman or no—did it with much more elegance.

"Ah, fair lady," Percy began in his precise, high-pitched tones. "I beg of you, grant your most obedient servant a few more precious minutes of your company and stand up with me again for the quadrille just forming."

She curtsied in reply. "Certainly, good sire. I am honoured by Your Majesty's condescension."

Percy actually giggled. Did she sound like that? She wouldn't do it again! She accepted his arm and allowed him to lead her past the frustrated Pontleby.

How overblown and artificial Percy's words and actions seemed. He lacked the grace of her impossible masked man, but he at least could be counted on to keep the line! He was a gentleman. Never would he dare attempt more than that chaste kissing of her fingertips. She firmly repressed a feeling of regret. She must give Percy his due. He might look ridiculous in his costume, but he tripped a truly light fantastic and could be counted on never to miss a step. Dependable, her father called him, and yes, he was. But not romantic...

What was she thinking? *Romantic? Ridiculous!* For a fleeting moment a truly romantic figure came to mind, one with a mask and a swirl of crimson-lined cape. Foolish play-actors, both of them . . . and only one suited to the part. She returned Percy's opening bow with a hurried curtsy as the orchestra struck up the tune.

Henry Pontleby was searching for her again when the dance came to an end. She had now stood up twice with Percy, and could not do so again without confirming the rumours already going the rounds, as well as giving Percy false hopes.

"Pray excuse me, Percy," she said quickly. "I must speak to my godmama at once. I—I have a message for her from Papa."

Not waiting for his profuse offers to escort her, she dodged behind a portly lady and quickly made her way to the other end of the room. Here rout chairs had been placed in a row along the wall for chaperons and matrons. Amelia Robertshaw was there. Juliana paused before she drew near. A tall gentleman dressed as a well-padded version of Henry VIII engaged her hostess in conversation.

He turned, looking directly at Juliana, and spoke to her godmama. Lady Robertshaw leaned past him, glanced at her, and nodded.

RANCE'S FIRST MOVE on returning to the ballroom in his new guise was to locate his hostess and apologize abjectly for his late arrival. His second was to beg of her the identity of the young lady dressed in wine velvet.

"Ah, you mean our Portia. That is Miss Juliana Beveridge, the daughter of Sir Agramont."

"Indeed? Then I believe I know her father." And know him for an unconscionable old reprobate, he added to himself. "So that is Beveridge's girl. Will you not grant me an introduction?"

Lady Robertshaw led him the few steps to Miss Beveridge's side and, from the corner of his eye, Rance saw Henry Pontleby bearing down upon her purposefully. Now there was a man he wouldn't wish his sister to know, had he a sister. He turned so that he blocked the girl from Pontleby's sight, feeling oddly protective towards the intrepid young female.

Lady Robertshaw was speaking. "Juliana, my love, allow me to make you acquainted with an old friend of mine, the Marquis of Ranceford. My lord, this is Miss Juliana Beveridge, who is my goddaughter." She beamed on them both. "My dear, may I present him as a partner for the country dance now forming?"

Rance bowed over Juliana's hand, affording her a clear view of Pontleby's approach. "Will you honour me, Miss Beveridge, by standing up with me for this next dance?"

She gave him a disinterested murmur and hurriedly accepted the arm he offered, her eyes on the disgruntled Pontleby. This would not do. Rance wanted her to look at him, that he might ascertain any spark of recognition.

"I believe I know your father," he said, prompting her.

This caught her attention. "Know *of* him, you mean," she answered, and immediately glanced up, rueful. "I beg your pardon. I should not have answered so. Forgive my unruly tongue."

"No, indeed. In fact, you may be right."

Her mouth snapped shut and she curtsied stiffly as they took their places in the set.

He addressed several remarks to her whenever they came together in the movements of the dance, using his normal voice and assuming a haughty manner suitable to a marquis and not a romantic Corsair. She remained coldly distant, her feet automatically performing the familiar steps, quite ignoring the man at her side, while her eyes strayed constantly to the French windows opening onto the terrace.

Rance began to relax. Obviously, she did not connect the Marquis of Ranceford with her masked admirer. As the dance concluded, he returned her to Lady Robertshaw, bowing deeply, and the girl dismissed him as though without a second thought.

Secure in the knowledge that she had not penetrated his disguise, Rance began to enjoy himself. He leaned against a wall, watching the peregrinations of Henry Pontleby and one Percival Woffington Netherfield, a man whom he knew slightly. Pontleby attempted several times to corner Miss Beveridge, while Netherfield acted the dog in the manger, as though the girl belonged to him. By far the better choice, Rance felt, amused. But not a man of great intelligence, he noted a moment later. Netherfield placed the girl on a chair near the chaperons and departed to obtain refreshments from the drawing-room. Pontleby closed in at once and Rance, with no conscious decision, moved in behind him in time to hear her reply.

"Sir, I have stood up with you twice already and twice with Mr. Netherfield, and I will not take the floor a third time with any man. I have no desire to furnish the gossip-mongers with more grist for their mills."

"Then you must be heated with so much dancing." Pontleby bent over her, his voice low and persuasive. "It is cool on the terrace. Let us step outside for a breath of fresh air." He reached for her. She drew back in her chair and he caught her hand, trying to pull her to her feet.

Enough of this. Rance stepped in with an elegant bow. "Pardon, Miss Beveridge, but I believe the contredanse you promised me is now forming. Have you forgotten?"

For only a second, a startled flicker crossed her face. Then, removing her hand from Pontleby's grasp, she rose smoothly. "Indeed, my lord, I did not realize. I must thank you for remembering." She accepted his arm and gave it a slight, grateful pressure.

They spoke only polite inanities as they danced, and still she gave no sign of recognizing him as the Corsair. Neither did she show the least indication of interest. That in itself intrigued Ranceford, who was accustomed to countless lures cast his way by young ladies determined to end his bachelorhood.

Which reminded him that he had promised Clara to stand up with both the Robertshaw daughters, and their mother would certainly report his every action to Clara, who was awake on every suit. He grinned as he guided Miss Beveridge through the final measures. What would his single-minded sister-in-law make of his dancing twice with this impecunious and untitled miss? He could be sure a series of social engagements involving Lady Catherine Moffet would commence immediately upon her return, if not sooner.

He made his final bow to his partner, and found himself comparing her critically to his sister-in-law's entry to the field. No contest. Lady Catherine's cold, proud features ran a poor second to the lively, decisive countenance which constantly turned not to him, but to the French windows. His pulses quickened. She might think the masked Corsair ridiculous, but he was evidently not forgotten.

To his relief, for Pontleby still hovered, Miss Beveridge took her leave of her hostess and left the ballroom as soon as their dance was over. Rance himself, after standing up with good grace with each of the young Robertshaws, quit the ball as well. With something of the sensation of having performed a death-defying feat and survived, he called for his curricle, feeling secure in the knowledge that his masquerade was safe from discovery. That intrepid damsel was out of his life forever. For which he should give thanks fasting! If only he could be sure she chose Netherfield and not Pontleby... But why should he feel uneasy about a female so capable of taking care of herself? Oddly, he did....

As Ranceford turned his curricle through the gates of the rhododendron-lined drive leading to the mews behind his house, a dark figure materialized out of the shadows and rose up before him in the moonlight. Startled, he jobbed at the reins and his greys reared in the traces. It took him a few seconds to recognize the bandaged head of One-eye Willyum. He settled his horses and stared.

The moonlight revealed a fascinating sight. His man, Beasley, had followed the instructions regarding refurbishing the highwayman to the letter. Willyum now sported the stained hunting coat and scuffed, once-white-topped boots in which Rance had spent an uncomfortable few minutes in a muddy drainage ditch on the other side of the tall hedge bounding his property in Leicestershire. The black satin knee-breeches on which he had spilled salmon mayonnaise at a Carlton House party hung nearly to Willy's ankles. With an exclamation of annoyance, Rance recognized a flowered waistcoat he was particularly fond of, but of which his valet had actively disapproved.

One-eye Willyum, however, was bursting with pride. He came bounding up as soon as the curricle came to a halt and his life was no longer in danger from flailing hooves.

"'Oy there, me lord!" he shouted. "Cast your daylights over 'ere! Ain't I bang up to the mark? Near as naught took me for one o' the nibs, they did, back at the ol' Nag's 'Ead."

Ranceford was speechless.

Willyum climbed up on a wheel and bent on him a closer look. "Stap me vittels, I'd never 'ave knowed yer, lessen it 'ad ter be yer acomin' in 'ere at a gallop. 'Oo yer bein' now?" He didn't wait for an answer. "Not 'arf betwattled, they was, when they seen me. Ast where I left the corpse." He roared with delight.

Raising his quizzing glass, Rance inspected the repellant sight again. He shuddered, but was not one to curdle another's cream pot. "You are indeed a regular pink of the ton," he told the happy man. "Did you lie in wait here to show me your, ah, glorification?"

Willyum dropped from his precarious perch on one of the spokes of the wheel. "I begs pardon fer stoppin' yer, me lord." He brushed off the front of Rance's former hunting coat. "Wot yer g'me afore settled me accounts at the inn, but in all me new clothes, I've a mind to 'ave a roost o' me own and not doss down w' a packet o' ramshackle cutpurses and dabbler dips."

He looked up at Rance with a self-righteous smirk. "Yer wouldn't want fer me to get rolled up by some o' them canters now I'm taking' the straight road."

Rance shook his head. "Straight? That I'll never believe."

Willyum took on the injured look of a spanked puppy. "I swear it, me lord, on me father's grave."

"I doubt you even know who he is." With a sigh of resignation, Rance drew a few silver coins from his pocket and dropped them into Willyum's outstretched hand.

"Thanks be ter yer, me lord. I disremember when I've met a rummer cove! G'me a word an yer ever need a 'elpin' 'and."

Rance hesitated. There might be a way the man would be of use. He had no real hope—or desire—of receiving a request for rescue from Miss Beveridge, but if she should ever send for him . . .

"Willyum, there is a chance, albeit a thin one, that a message for me from a lady may come to the Nag's Head in your name. It will be addressed to Conrad, or maybe just to the Corsair."

"The wot?"

Rance, already sorry he'd mentioned it, gathered up his reins. "A corsair is a sort of pirate."

Willyum nodded sagely. "There be good pickin's on the Thames. I knows of a bloke—"

"Yes, well, never mind." Rance gave his pair the office and the curricle moved on.

"Don't yer be afeared, me lord!" Willyum yelled after him. "I'll be on the watch fer it and I knows where to find yer."

Rance pulled up short and leaned out to shout back. "Not a word about tonight's affair, for God's sake!"

"Me chaffers mum," answered the little highwayman with a cheery wave. "Aw rivwar!"

Au revoir, indeed. Rance realized he'd acquired a pensioner. Oh, the devil. He'd certainly see the man again—and again. One-eye Willyum knew who he really was.

SIR AGRAMONT, keeping unaccustomed early hours, was already home and having a nightcap in the library when Juliana and Emily Jane were deposited at the door by a sleepy John Coachman. He poked his head out into the hall.

"Home, eh?" he greeted his daughter. "Enjoy yourself? Come in and tell me all."

Juliana dismissed the yawning Emily Jane, who had so far forgot herself as to sleep all the way home. She joined her father. Two padded chairs were set before the hearth in which a small fire still smouldered.

"I daresay you've danced all evening," Sir Agramont began, seating himself. "No doubt Percy was there."

Juliana curled up in the other chair, tucking her feet beneath her skirt. "Can you doubt it, Papa? He came as Louis XIV. I wish you may have seen him! The poor king must have spun in his grave."

Sir Agramont coughed. "Percy is a good man, puss. Have you thought more on his offer?"

"Oh, yes, and came to the same decision. I could not spend my life with such a clodpole."

Her father twisted uncomfortably in his chair. "Did you by chance meet Mr. Henry Pontleby there?"

"Yes. As seldom as possible."

He glanced at her. His gaze slid evasively away. "Do you not think him an excellent gentleman?"

"Pontleby?" Juliana was astounded. "He is not such a gentleman as you think."

"Well now, puss. You must forgive him if he seems a trifle forward. I have to tell you that he wishes to fix his interest with you."

"Is that what he was attempting to do?"

Sir Agramont eyed her anxiously. "He is very good ton. And his person is all that is agreeable. If you will not have Percy, could you not consider Pontleby?"

Juliana stood up abruptly. "Papa, I wish you'd cease trying to find husbands for me."

"Only one, my dear, I promise you. But we must wed you to a rich man while you still have your beauty. Your face is our fortune, you must know."

"Papa, I am going to my bed."

He scrambled to his feet, catching her arm. "Juliana, I fear we cannot wait. You must either marry Percy's fortune or accept Pontleby's offer before the month is out."

She stopped and faced him, stunned. "Whatever do you mean? Papa, tell me. What have you done now?"

Sir Agramont's face puckered like a child's about to cry. "The man had the devil's own luck, puss. Were he not a gentleman, I'd suspect the dice were uphills."

Coming back to her chair, Juliana sank into it. She felt she could no longer stand. "Out with it, Papa. Let's have the tale with no roundaboutation."

She listened in silence while the words fairly tumbled from Sir Agramont's trembling lips. Gaming, as she suspected, and he had lost a prodigious amount to Pontleby. The man held his vowels and demanded either payment within the month or his daughter's hand.

"Papa, how much are you in his debt?"

Sir Agramont quoted a sum which caused Juliana to turn white. Numb with shock, she rose silently and went up to her chamber.

She lay in her bed, at her wit's end and unable to close her eyes. If only there were some way to get those dreadful vowels back from Pontleby. Insidiously, the image of the masked man crept into her mind. She remembered his nonsensical claim to be a rescuer of damsels in distress. How much more distressed could a damsel be? It was the very devil that he was a modern man and only play-acting, now when she felt catapulted into a Gothic novel.

But suppose he was serious . . . suppose he really meant it? It was only a straw, but she grasped it. There was no other way to turn. What she needed was a daring hero, one who would break into Pontleby's home and steal her father's vowels before she must submit to a Fate Worse Than Death. Adorinda might faint, but not Juliana. Not before all roads were tried.

Slipping out of bed, she lighted a candle on her writing desk. With the tip of her tongue protruding slightly between her lips, she bent her mind to composing a suitable missive. She addressed it to Conrad the Corsair, to be delivered by the hand of One-eye Willyum at the Nag's Head Inn.

CHAPTER FOUR

JULIANA HAD SPENT the better part of an hour on her message to the masked man before finally achieving a passing epistle, but as she read it over in the uncompromising light of day, she was assailed by misgivings. What if he did not answer? Would he even get her call for help? He might not have meant what he said; perhaps he only played an amusing game. He spoke as a gentleman, and gentlemen, notoriously, were prone to cutting larks. It was no doubt all a hoax. He must have made up the tale of One-eye Willyum. Surely no one would have such a name.

She curled up, despondent, in the window-seat of her bedchamber and stared down into the street below, blind to the early-morning traffic, until a carriage stopped at her door. Odd, her father had few callers and none at such an hour. He might not have left his room, let alone eaten his breakfast.

A man descended from the coach and she leaned over for a better look. Pontleby! She shrank back behind the curtains. Whatever could the man want? Had he come to demand payment before the month was out? She knew a sinking of the hot chocolate and buns on which she'd breakfasted. Good grief, suppose he had come to offer for her again in place of cash payment for those awful vowels? She had little faith in her father's ability to say no.

Hardly had ten minutes passed when Emily Jane poked her head in the door.

"Your papa wants you, Miss Julie. In the bookroom."

Juliana knew her worst fear answered. What could she do? Faint like Adorinda, and accomplish no earthly good? She would *not* be an hysterical Gothic heroine... but neither did she wish to submit to a horrid fate.

"Tell—tell him I'm not coming down."

Emily Jane's eyes grew even rounder. "Oo, Miss Julie, not me."

"All right, I'll rephrase that. Tell him I told you to say I'm not coming down."

"But there's another gentleman with 'im. One 'as wants to see you."

"Well, he shan't."

"But, Miss Julie—"

Juliana, her nerves already on edge, lost her patience. "Oh, Emily Jane, do not be such a caper-wit! I do not wish to see that gentleman. Go back down and tell my father I am unable to leave my chamber. I am indisposed. Tell him the chicken pâté at the ball must have been off."

"Yus'm." But the abigail looked dubious.

And Juliana felt dubious as well. It would not serve. She could not stay indisposed forever. The time had come when she'd have to choose, and quickly, between Pontleby and Percival Woffington Netherfield. A lowering thought. The lesser evil was Percy. He'd have to be her first choice. Or did she have a third? There was only one way to find out, but there was a slight problem. How was a delicately nurtured young female to deliver a message to a bawdy tavern? The masked man had specifically ordered her not to go there herself. Emily Jane, however, was not all that delicate, and John Coachman had known Juliana from her cradle. Those two were the only persons beside herself who knew of her masked man's existence. And she could count on them.

Emily Jane was already out in the hall, and Juliana ran after her. "Wait! When you've seen my father, come back here. I need you."

Emily Jane turned. "Coo, Miss Julie, 'ave you come over all queer for true?"

"Of course not, feather-head. But it won't hurt to have Papa think so. You must help me with something."

"Coo," said Emily Jane again, her face lighting up. "Be we goin' to take 'is other dressing-gown?"

"Certainly not. No such thing. We already did that and we must not repeat ourselves. This will be different. Now hurry."

Delighted at the prospect of another game afoot, Emily Jane hurried.

Juliana read her note to the masked man yet again, her spirits lifting. Yes, it would do—always providing there *was* a One-eye Willyum.

Going to her writing desk, she folded the sheet of paper so that none of the message could be seen and held her stick of wax to the candle. She dribbled it over the raw edge. Then, as an afterthought, she sealed the sides as well. Sir Agramont had once given her a very pretty stamp, embossed with a rose, but she wanted no betraying clues to her identity in the hands of a thief. She mashed the wax flat with the handle of her hairbrush. Emily Jane returned as she finished printing the direction on the outside.

"This must be kept secret," she told the abigail, who turned pink with excitement. "I want it delivered to the Nag's Head Inn in Covent Garden, and John Coachman is to go with you."

Emily Jane could read simple printing if no one pressed her. Her lips moved as she sounded out the letters. "'Oo's this One-eye Willyum?"

Juliana spoke without thinking. "He is the highwayman I brained with John Coachman's gun."

"Coo!" said Emily Jane. "And oo's this Conrad?"

She could never keep secrets from Emily Jane. It was better in the long run not to try, because the persistent girl, like a truffle pig, would eventually root out any tidbit which intrigued her. She gave up. "Our masked rescuer."

"Coo." Emily Jane breathed her favourite word, her eyes sparkling. "One o' them love billy doos, ain't it?"

Juliana felt her cheeks flush. "It is certainly not a billet-doux! Merely a thank-you note for rescuing us from the hold-up."

"I'm thinkin' it was you rescued 'im."

"I know, but gentlemen don't like to be told that. It's better if he thinks I think he did it." She had come up with a lovely excuse for contacting him! Juliana felt quite proud of herself. "Naturally, I would send him my thanks."

Emily Jane smirked. "Yus, you would," she said. "Don't think I didn't guess it was 'im at that party last night. I seen you w'yer 'air in a muss."

Juliana's lips tightened. "One of these days you'll go too far, my girl. Now take this and find John Coachman. And, Emily Jane..."

Chastened, the abigail lowered her eyes. "Yus, Miss Julie?"

"Do be careful. It is not a nice place, and I don't want anything to happen to you."

Emily Jane beamed like a puppy who had expected a spanking and received a pat on the head. She grinned and would have wagged her tail had she one. "Don't you be worriting about me, Miss Julie. I'll 'ave John Coachman and I'll stick right to 'im like a court plaster."

"Well, see that you do."

Emily Jane winked at her, in another breach of decorum, as she tucked the note in her apron pocket. Prey to no little anxiety, Juliana watched her trot down the hall towards the back stairs, and then went herself to her favourite window-seat.

She could do nothing now but wait.

THE MARQUIS OF RANCEFORD awoke that morning with a problem of his own. His Corsair costume was soaked and slimy, but he was not about to give it up if he could help it. He had carried it to his rooms rolled in his curricle blanket, and the bundle now lay on the floor of his wardrobe, far in the back.

Beasley entered, bearing a pot of tea and a cup on a tray. Rance considered the man who had been with him since his schooldays. If one couldn't trust one's valet . . .

"About my costume, Beasley," he began.

"Yes, my lord." The valet deposited the tray on the bedside table with the care and elegance of one proffering a crown to a king. "I have already taken the liberty of sending Robert to return the Henry VIII apparel to the costumier."

"Ah . . . no. That is, I didn't wear only that one."

"No, my lord?" Beasley waited, respectfully at attention.

"No, I also went as an entirely different character."

"Indeed, my lord."

"Yes, and, ah, I had a slight accident." In a rush, he added, "I seem to have fallen in a pond."

One of Beasley's eyebrows raised. "Dear me, if I may say so, my lord."

Rance slid out of bed and unlocked the wardrobe. He pulled out the blanket, unrolling the sodden Corsair outfit on the rug.

Beasley eyed it with something approaching revulsion. "Dear me," he said again.

"Can this rig be cleaned? I—I might want to wear it again some time."

"Certainly, my lord." The valet lifted a corner of the cape, sniffed at it, and dropped it back on the blanket before rolling up the whole affair. "I shall take care of it at once, my lord."

"And, Beasley—"

"Yes, my lord?"

"I'd rather Lady Clara knew nothing of this."

Beasley's lips twitched. "Naturally, my lord." He hesitated before going out the door. "Might I ask, has this anything to do with the person to whom I gave some of your old garments last night?"

"Well, in a way."

The man nodded. "If I may make so bold, it is about time your lordship had a bit of a lark."

He left, carrying the rolled blanket at arm's length, and Ranceford picked up his teacup.

Several long hours later, the Marquis of Ranceford emerged from his study after a tedious business session with his bailiff, who had ridden in from his country estate. He paused in the hall, stretched cramped shoulders, and twisted a kink out of his back. A waste of time: the man could handle all by himself. Why did he not simply present the papers for signatures? Why sit there with a blank expression, waiting for him to read them all through?

With a rueful grin, he realized why he himself would do the same, were he in Hodder's shoes. Naturally, the man resented Rance's lack of interest in his vast lands. But how could he be expected to enthuse over what would one day become the property of a man he had never met? As matters now lay, a distant cousin stood to inherit all. Meanwhile, the current Marquis of Ranceford merely sat in stewardship. It was not as if Rance had a son for whom to preserve his land... His thoughts moved along a familiar road. Life had been different while David had lived, when his brother might have yet begot an heir, and it had mattered not a jot if he himself had never felt the urge to become leg-shackled. And still he did not. He was damned if Clara would force him to wed and start his nursery in order to ensure her own tenancy. Better the unknown cousin.

Jobbins the butler walked with dignity across the hall in front of him and threw open the double front doors. Lady Clara, who had just descended from her carriage, came up the front stairs. She saw Rance and began talking as she entered the house.

"Ranceford, I have just come from paying a morning call on Amelia Robertshaw to learn the news of her ball." She struggled with the buttons of her new azure velvet pelisse as she mounted the broad curving staircase towards her chamber. "It is excessively warm, travelling in that enclosed carriage. I do wish you would procure a new open landau. I am quite ashamed to appear in the old one. I have requested a light nuncheon to be laid out in the breakfast parlour. Please join me there, for I wish to speak with you." Typically, she swept upward without awaiting his answer.

Rance shrugged. His conscience was clear—well, reasonably so. She could not know of the exciting events of the evening, and his behaviour at the ball had been exemplary. He wandered into the designated room, sat down at the table, and began to peel a peach with a delicate silver knife. He consumed two, a jam tartlet and a lemon cream while he waited. She finally arrived, now garbed in a puce faille round gown, with a frilly blond lace cap on her fashionably cropped curls. She went at once to the sideboard where she peered under the covers of several chafing dishes. Ever an excellent trencherwoman, as testified by her waistline, she filled her plate before speaking.

"Amelia tells me you arrived very late at her ball last night."

Rance raised his eyebrows. "Your friend must have been inattentive." He toyed with the silver knife. "I was there. I might have visited the card room for a few hands of picquet before dancing. She wouldn't have seen me."

Lady Clara set down her fork. "I should think you'd get enough of that at your deplorable clubs. Balls are meant for dancing."

"Yes, when there is anyone with whom one wishes to dance."

"At least you came home at a decent hour." She switched to the topic which interested her. "Amelia was most pleased to see you stand up with both her girls." She glanced at him and back down at her plate, her manner entirely too casual. "I hear you extended your duties to include her goddaughter. For two dances." Another sidelong glance came his way.

"What? Oh, you must mean the Beveridge girl." His insouciance equalled hers. Picking up a plate, he wandered over to the sideboard and selected a thick slice of Westphalian ham.

Lady Clara waited with her ears pricked up, like a cat spotting a mouse. Rance could literally feel her tensing for the pounce. He wondered if he could fit through that hole he could see at the base of the wainscotting. No. He sighed.

"Pontleby was after her," he explained. "I merely came to her rescue." And this time, with better success. He gave himself a mental pat on the back.

"That man!" Temporarily distracted, Lady Clara chewed rapidly and swallowed a mouthful of muffin-and-jam. "And to think my Augusta will be out this very next Season. I certainly hope you will drop a few words in his ear, Ranceford. I'll not have the likes of him dangling after one of my girls!"

Not much chance of that, Rance thought, seating himself at the table with his plate. All five were bran-faced, carrot-topped and had more hair than wit. Except possibly little Mirabella. Even so, he'd have to stand buff for five substantial dowries if he was to empty his house. He wondered how much blunt it would take to get off a fortyish widow....

The fortyish widow was still talking. "But that is neither here nor there. I must tell you that Ethelinda and Mirabella are both taken with the measles and I have the greatest fears for Augusta, Rosamund and Ophelia. The dear girls wish to go to Astley's Amphitheatre to see the Grand Equestrian Exhibition tomorrow evening before they, too, may break out in the rash. I want you to escort us."

"They've *been* to Astley's." He stabbed at his ham, annoyed.

"It's an entirely new show, and I've promised them a treat. If you have another engagement, Ranceford, you must cancel it."

Rance reminded himself firmly that this was David's widow. David's children. The least he could do for his dead brother. Five years... and the wound of his loss was still raw. No doubt aggravated by Clara's constant irritation. He dismissed that cynical thought.

"Very well," he said quietly, and cut off a mouthful of ham. But, oh, he dreamed as he chewed, to be chasing the muslim Pacha across a boundless sea and rescuing a dusky-haired Gulnare, instead of shepherding a bevy of schoolgirls to a boring horse show.

He became aware of his butler standing by his left elbow and making soft throat-clearing noises, his expression much like that of Beasley's when inspecting the pond-damaged Corsair costume.

"Yes, Jobbins. What is it?"

"A person, my lord. He desires to see your lordship and refuses to go away."

"A person? What person?" Rance guessed from Jobbin's tone that it was not a member of the ton.

"He said, my lord, that if the name Conrad was mentioned, you would wish to see him at once."

Oh, the devil! Rance forgot his ham. Now what did One-eye Willyum want? It had to be him—no one else knew. A warning bell clanged in the back of his mind. Was he to be blackmailed by the cozening rascal? If he should talk... But with a touch of relief, Rance remembered that One-eye Willyum was hardly likely to travel in the same circles as the Marquis of Ranceford.

"Conrad?" demanded Lady Clara, breaking into his reverie. "Who is this Conrad?"

"A—a friend of mine." Rance thought quickly and prevaricated. "He owes me some money. No doubt this is an envoy sent to beg more time." Dropping his napkin, he rose to his feet. "Where is he, Jobbins? I'll see him."

"Gaming," Clara sniffed. "I'd demand payment at once, if I were you, Ranceford. Teach the man a lesson."

That I shall, he swore grimly to himself. The little weasel would not hold him up a second time. Or did this make a third? And where could he see him in privacy? No telling what the clodpole might say aloud. "Ah—show him into my study, Jobbins."

A few minutes later, decked in all his new finery, One-eye Willyum appeared at the study door, escorted by the disapproving butler. Willy, his face wreathed in smiles, held out a grimy twist of paper.

"'Ere yer are, me lord. Came right as yer said."

Rance sat down suddenly in his desk chair. "What?"

"Yer billy-doo from that gentry mort wot 'it me."

With a hand that shook, Rance accepted the bit of folded paper. Although a trifle the worse for wear, the writing on the outside was legible—and in a clearly feminine hand. "One-eye Willyum," he read. "To be delivered by hand to Conrad the Corsair." His fingers were all thumbs as he broke the seals and spread out the sheet.

My dear sir,

If you meant what you said on the Robertshaws' terrace last night, have the goodness to meet me at the foot of the garden behind Beveridge House tonight at midnight. I find I am in dire need and would greatly appreciate it if you could come to my aid in a most pressing matter.

Portia.

Rance looked up; his butler still waited inside the door, his ears perked like a terrier hoping for a bone. Damn the man! It wouldn't do to have this story repeated belowstairs. Reaching into his pocket, he removed a couple of flimsies from his roll of soft. This was no time for half-crowns. He handed a bill to each of the men.

"You will not speak of this or I wash my hands of you both. Jobbins, show Mr., ah, Willyum out, and send Beasley to me at once."

Alone again, Rance leaned back in his chair, a thrill of excitement racing through his veins. His damsel was once more in distress and she had sent for the Corsair! But what of his costume? Had Beasley been able to save it?

He had. Beasley, answering his summons, reassured him. "I have already sponged the garments, my lord, though I fear I was unable to entirely remove the aroma. They are even now spread to dry before a strong fire in your lordship's bedchamber."

"Thank you, Beasley!" Rance almost peeled off another flimsy, but caught himself before he insulted his man. But there would be a bonus attached to Beasley's salary this quarter.

Tonight. This very night, Conrad the Corsair would ride once more.

AND RIDE HE DID, but in a staid fashion, seated in his curricle with his caped driving coat hiding his Corsair costume. As soon as he felt safe from curious eyes, he turned about and headed for the Coach and Horses in Smithfield. He needed to collect that dratted horse in order to make a properly dashing entrance. After all, he was promised a real quest, an unhoped-for adventure. And he'd no intention of making a mull of it this time.

He wiggled his toes. His boots had not dried at all. His breeches were decidedly clammy about the crotch and waistband, the lower edge of his cape swung damply, but all in all his outfit was passable. Perhaps a slight odour of pond weed clung about him, but they would be out of doors. The garden, she had said. Who would notice another smell among the scents of flowers and loam?

His clothes might be uncomfortable, but he couldn't care less. He was the Corsair. He rode to the rescue of a fair maiden, and he'd best hurry if he meant to get there before she cracked another skull.

CHAPTER FIVE

JULIANA KNEW a most worrisome day. Ever since Emily Jane had reported that there actually was a One-eye Willyum and he knew all about Conrad the Corsair, she had been in a fever of impatience.

"I saw Mr. Willyum, Miss Julie," the maid enthused. "A grand man, 'e is in 'is fancy rig. Not like when 'e 'eld us hup in 'is 'ighwayman disguise. Promised to deliver your billy-doo immediate, 'e did."

"I told you it was *not* a billet-doux, Emily Jane. A thank-you note, that is all."

The abigail grinned. "Yus'm. Be you goin' to meet 'im somewheres?"

Juliana hesitated. It might be best to take Emily Jane into her confidence, at least partway. Getting out of the house at midnight presented no great problem, but suppose Conkley, doing his butlerian duty, made a final check on the doors and windows, locking her out? She would have need of a loyal ally. She studied Emily Jane, who was as excited as an eager puppy, and suddenly realized that the girl was the only person in the world whom she felt she could trust. The only person really close to her, one she could depend on to stick by her through thick and thin. And life, she decided, had become about as thick as it could get.

She sat down on the edge of her bed and gestured towards her dressing-table stool.

"Sit down, Emily Jane."

"Coo, miss, I couldn't!"

"Yes, you can, Emily Jane. This is just between us and you must never breath a word of this to anyone."

The abigail sat, her eyes round and cheeks glowing with earnestness. "Me chaffers mum, Miss Julie."

"Your what?"

"That's what Mr. One-eye Willyum said when I gives 'im the letter. It means I swear never to tell."

This was good enough for Juliana, who knew her own chaffer to be far from mum. She had to tell someone. The story of Sir Agramont's vowels and Henry Pontleby's villainous proposal for their redemption came bubbling out, the words tumbling over each other, while Emily Jane sat transfixed.

"I vow, it's like one of those ridiculous Gothic novels," Juliana finished. "Mr. Pontleby is my Count Valnescue."

"'Oo's 'e?"

Juliana picked up her copy of *Adorinda* and tossed it to her. "It's in there, in this book I've been reading. The heroine is kidnapped by an evil man, who plans to force her to wed him, only, of course, she will be saved by her hero, Lord Eduardo."

"Yer masked man." Emily Jane sighed, ecstatic. "Only 'is name is Conrad. D'yer fancy 'e'll come to yer rescue?"

"He may be my only hope."

Emily Jane turned the pages of the book she held. "This 'ere Eduardo, 'ow does 'e save 'is poppet?"

Juliana let her designation of Adorinda's character pass. "I don't know yet. That is only volume 2. There's one more before the story ends."

"Oo, miss. We'd best find out 'ow 'e did it. So's you can tell yer masked man."

The situations in the novel and her life were not quite the same, but Juliana knew a curiosity she had not felt before as to how Lord Eduardo managed the rescue of his hen-witted Adorinda. Emily Jane was sent off to Hookam's to procure volume 3.

The afternoon passed more quickly than Juliana had hoped. The two girls pored over Adorinda's tale, Juliana reading aloud significant bits to an entranced Emily Jane. Eduardo's solution, however, they did not deem practical, for in the next-to-last chapter, the heroic lord found it necessary to free his love by hacking Count Valnescue to bits with his own sword. That would not do. The laws of modern London prohibited such actions. The masked man would have to find some other means.

The dinner hour came and went. As midnight drew near, Juliana trembled with anticipation. Would he come? And if he did, would the outrageous man have the temerity to kiss her again when he met her alone—

vulnerable—in the dark of the garden? Oh, but she hoped he would! The man was delightfully dangerous!

Shocked at herself, she tried to sort out her tumultuous thoughts. Certainly, she meant to ask his aid in retrieving her father's vowels, but being honest, she admitted that to be secondary. First and foremost, her treacherous fancies revolved about the kiss on the terrace. The strength of his arms as he had held her, helpless, against his broad chest...warm, firm lips sliding across her cheek and finding hers...a gentle touch, then deepening, arousing a rush of warm sensations she'd never dreamt possible.... And she had kissed him back.

Never had there been such a kiss. Pontleby had tried to kiss her once. She shuddered. How could she pair the two men in the same thought?

At five minutes to midnight, wrapped in her darkest pelisse, Juliana prepared to tiptoe from the house. She had a bit of trouble with Emily Jane, who wanted to come along, but she finally managed to convince the girl that it was her duty to stand guard by the side door to the garden. When Emily Jane found she was to hide behind the curtains when her Uncle Conkley came to lock up and then slip out and undo the bolt for Miss Juliana, she agreed to stay behind.

"Give 'im one in the eye that will," she explained to her mistress. "'Im 'oo thinks 'e's so smart."

Having mounted her rearguard, Juliana slipped out and made her way towards the back garden. Everything looked different at night. A cloud obscured the moon and familiar trees and shrubs took on unusual shapes and seemed to reach for her with twiggy fingers as she passed. Luckily, she was not fanciful. No footpads—or worse, spectres—lurked in the Beveridge pleasuance. Her feet began to run of their own volition, and by the time she reached the stone bench by the lake at the foot of the garden, her heart pounded so that it must be audible to anyone near.

That was not her heart! Hoofbeats—had he come? A sudden fear assailed her. Suppose he thought she sent for him because she wanted him to kiss her again? What would he do? Adorinda always fainted when about to be seduced, which seemed an addlepated thing to do—or should she try? But it was too late.

He rode up on a dancing steed, his face masked and a sword at his side. At the entrance to the rose garden, he dismounted in a swirl of crimson-lined cape and secured his horse to the leg of a life-sized statue of Prometheus, conveniently handy. He strode towards her, his cape billowing about him; the cloud passed from the moon and its light glinted on white teeth as he smiled.

Sweeping a magnificent leg, he bowed over her hand, kissing only her fingertips. Relief mingled with a touch of disappointment as the dark night became a beautiful, star-filled arena and the shadows fled. A soft breeze ruffled her hair. It seemed, she noted, sniffing, to be coming from the reed-edged shore of the lake.

She pressed a hand to her heart to still its wild beating. "You've come," she exclaimed, her voice low and throbbing. Good grief, she was acting just like Adorinda!

He went down on one knee, still smiling. "Fair lady, could you doubt me?" He rose. "Now," he asked in a normal tone, "what's all this about being in dire need? How may I serve you?"

Juliana came down to earth with a bump. This was more like, she told herself. Enough of Gothic foolishness! It was good fun, but her problem was real and immediate. Suddenly she panicked. How could she explain to this strange man what she wished him to do? What could she say?

"You said you had need of me," he prompted.

There was only one way to enter an ice-cold bath. Plunge right in. She drew a deep breath.

"Yes, I—oh, I wish you were a real masked hero and could leap to my rescue, but that only happens in novels."

"Try me." He smiled down at her, causing her pulse to beat faster. "Perhaps our novel will have a happy ending."

Juliana poised on the brink for only a moment before taking the leap. "Would you commit a crime for me to right a great wrong?"

He seemed taken aback, but recovered. "That depends on the crime. I do not much favour becoming a murderer, if that is what you have in mind."

"Oh, no. The man may live. A—a theft, merely."

"Merely?"

"But in a good cause!"

He took her hand, seating her on the stone bench and sitting beside her. His shoulder brushed hers, setting off a tingling awareness of his masculinity. She felt helpless, all feminine . . .

"You'd best tell me all before I am sentenced to hang," he suggested practically, breaking into her daze.

All. He was right. She gathered in her chaotic feelings and began her explanation in a rush. "First you must know that when my father dies, I shall be left penniless. I must marry a rich man."

He drew back, looking uneasy. "But Sir Agramont is not old. He will last for years."

"Yes, but I won't. I should be at least thirty when he passes on, and hopelessly on the shelf. I'd have to go as a nursemaid or a governess. That, however, is not to be my problem. My father is in need of a great deal of money—and quickly—so he wishes me to wed Percival Woffington Netherfield's fortune at once, and I quite despise him."

The masked man shook his head. "Then you must not consider it for an instant. What has brought on this sudden need of a vast sum?"

"A man named Henry Pontleby. He holds my father's vowels in the amount of several thousand pounds. I believe he may have cheated, using uphill dice. I cannot conceive of any other way he could have won so much from my father."

"I could."

She glanced at him sharply. Had he knowledge of her father's perennial ill luck? She hastened on with her tale. "Mr. Pontleby says Papa must either pay up by the end of the month or give him my hand in marriage. There is only one hope for me. Unless someone can steal back my father's vowels, I must marry a man I loathe or Pontleby will broadcast my father's failure to honour his debts like a gentleman. He will be blackballed in all the clubs."

"A good thing," the masked man interjected, as if he knew Sir Agramont personally.

"No, indeed," she exclaimed. "If that bit of news were to become common knowledge, our creditors would descend upon us like a flock of locusts, and we should be obliged to take up residence in Fleet Street."

The firm lips below the mask pursed. "I daresay that would be most uncomfortable. And it is Henry Pontleby who holds the vowels?" He reached over and patted her hand. "Do not give the matter another thought. I will settle all."

Almost, she believed he would. She turned to him impulsively, and might have kissed him in gratitude had he not suddenly risen to his feet. "You are leaving? But when shall I see you again?"

"Tomorrow night. Your troubles will be over. Oh, the devil," he added. "Not tomorrow. I must be at Astley's—that is, I have another engagement. I will meet you in two days' time, the vowels in hand, same place, same hour."

She rose also, and caught at his sleeve. Not only was she not to be seduced, he did not even plan to kiss her again! A series of negatives she meant to confute. She swayed towards him, holding up her face and closing her eyes. "How can I ever thank you?"

After a startled moment, he glanced behind him, as though checking for an ornamental pool. Then, the lake being a safe distance away, he proceeded to remedy his oversight. As his arms pressed her close against his warm, solid body, Juliana grew conscious of an odd feeling she could not identify, one only dimly remembered. She slid her own arms around his chest, as far as she could reach, drawing him to her. Then his gentle lips sought hers and she forgot all else in that incredible sensation of oneness, every bit as lovely as before.

He released her reluctantly, and strode towards his horse. His cape swirled about him, scaring the animal into rearing, but after a few tries he managed to climb into the saddle, and rode off into the shadows on his crow-hopping mount.

Juliana stood by the bench, the odd feeling gone, leaving her achingly bereft. She identified it then. *Comfort. Security.* Things she hadn't known since her earliest childhood. Within the arms of her masked hero, she had felt *safe* for the first time in the long years she'd spent in the custody of her erratic father. What was there about this strange man which made him seem so dependable, so capable? As though he really cared and would bend his every effort in her behalf?

Through a dark garden once more peopled with shadows, she walked back to the house where Emily Jane waited to let her in. She went slowly, for she had a new concept to consider. All her life, one belief had been drilled into her: the essential attributes of an eligible man were, in order, wealth, title, and consequence. A personable figure ran far back in the field. Why had her father not told her of humour, gentleness, comfort and safety? Indeed, she could just imagine Sir Agramont's opinions on *those* qualities. She'd certainly not meet with any of them in Henry Pontleby, nor would she find them if she wed Percy. Her whole future rested on the abilities of a ridiculously Gothic masked man.

RANCEFORD RODE OFF, his head in a whirl. *She* had kissed *him!* He had been wishing he dared kiss her again, but he was bred a gentleman with a strong sense of honour and, alone with him in the dark garden, the girl was quite in his power. Chivalry denied him the pleasure he longed for. He had known a moment of wild trepidation when she held up her face, patently expecting a kiss. He'd never meant to follow through—but he had. And *she* had kissed *him!*

At this point, the black horse shied at a shadow and nearly unseated him. He'd best get a grip on his emotions, as well as on that damnable horse, before he fell off. It was not a mount on which one could day-dream.

And yet, was it not a creature of his dreams? It typified all that he had imagined in the Corsair, an unwilling captive longing for freedom, headstrong and unreliable. He was beginning to feel actually fond of the mettlesome beast. It was a challenge, an adventure, every time he threw a leg over its saddle, and Rance was bored with his beautifully trained stable. On the black horse he was Conrad, and it was his enemy to be conquered. He should name it Pacha, after the arch-villain in *The Corsair*.

His teeth glinted again in the moonlight as he bared them in his best Conrad grin. Once you name an animal, it's an abbey to a Charly house that you intend to keep it. He'd meant to send the troublesome beast to Tatts' the very next day. Now, for the first time, he realized that he didn't want to give it up. That being the case, he'd best move his fractious mount from Smithfield to the Nag's Head for convenience's sake. One-eye Willyum could care for it and earn his keep. Neat, that. Solved two of his problems.

Getting back Sir Agramont's vowels he didn't consider a problem at all. There was, of course, only one way to handle the matter. He would have to buy them from Pontleby. Luckily, with his fortune, he would hardly notice the expense of a paltry few thousand pounds. His mind at rest, if not his seat, he continued on to the Coach and Horses to retrieve his curricle. He'd retrieve Pacha on the morrow.

Ordinarily, one of his grooms would have been sent to transfer the horse, but Rance treasured his secret alter ego. He drove his curricle to Smithfield the next day and hitched Pacha behind the equipage. Somehow, he made the move to the Nag's Head, having to pay for the damage to only one carriage door kicked in by the horse as they moved through the London traffic. He felt quite fortunate. And hungry. He proceeded on to White's for a leisurely luncheon, and there he encountered the very man he wished to see.

"Pontleby," he greeted him. "Won't you join me?"

The man looked surprised, as well he might, for he was not one of the marquis's select circle. Rance wasted no time in relieving his curiosity once they were seated with wine and a plate of rare beef.

"I understand you hold a packet of Beveridge's vowels. I would like to buy them from you if you'd care to sell."

He came up against a stumbling block. Pontleby smiled and shook his head.

"Not for sale, my lord. I have a far better use for them."

Indeed, Rance thought. *And I know what you intend, my fine fellow, but you're fair and far out there. She won't have you.* Aloud, he tried an inducement. "I have a fondness for the old gentleman. I'll pay a trifle over their value."

Alas, he was not cut out for bargaining; he'd had no practice. Rance knew at once he'd made a mistake when his opponent had recourse to his snuff-box before replying.

As he dusted off his sleeve, Pontleby leered. "Have your eye on the damsel, too, eh? I fear you must face disappointment. Find yourself another delectable morsel."

Ranceford's fists tightened into serviceable bunches of fives. Only with the greatest difficulty did he control an urge to draw Pontleby's cork and tap his claret right there in the centre of White's. Instead, he forced a smile over his clenched teeth. "I'll pay you double their worth." He knew before the words left his mouth that he had erred again.

Pontleby laughed outright. "You increase my anticipation, my lord." He leaned across the table and clapped Rance on the shoulder. "As one man of the world to another, I suggest you wait your turn. Meanwhile, join me at my digs Friday evening for cards. I can promise you some not contemptible cognac." He winked. "Courtesy of a friend."

Rance doubted he could speak without spitting. Alienating the man would do no good. In fact, whether he liked it or not, he'd best get closer to him. He'd no desire to foster such a friendship, but he'd have to find a way to get those vowels from him or face ignominious defeat. Unclenching his teeth by sheer force of will, he accepted the invitation.

AN HOUR LATER, as Rance approached his house, his front door swung open and James, the second footman, descended the stairs, pausing only for a brief bow before hotfooting it down the road with a folded sheet of paper in his hand. *Now* what was toward?

He soon discovered the reason. Lady Clara, fair to bursting with news, met him with a dramatic announcement as he stepped over the threshold.

"They are back!"

"What? The locusts?"

"Do be serious for once, Ranceford. I mean Lady Catherine Moffet and little Hubert, of course." She sounded more aggrieved than delighted. "The measles were all a hum. There is naught the matter with Hubert after all and dear Catherine missed the masquerade for nothing."

"Too bad." Even to himself his insincerity was obvious, but Clara's attention was elsewhere.

"I was so sure that dear Catherine was forced to go on a repairing lease to overcome the spots," she rambled on. "I did think that possibly it was poor little Hubert who gave the measles to Ethelinda and Mirabella, for they played together for the longest while in the park a fortnight ago. Be that as it may, it has all turned out for the best. I have just sent James or Robert—one of them—off to deliver an invitation to dear Catherine and little Hubert to join us in our box for the Grand Equestrian Exhibition at Astley's Amphitheatre this evening."

Hurrah, hurrah, Rance muttered to himself sourly as he let Jobbins relieve him of his driving coat. A fitting end to the day. He handed his hat and gloves to the butler and had a cheering thought. All might not be lost if the two Moffets had as yet avoided the measles. He had received the distinct impression after breakfast that both Augusta and Ophelia appeared rather flushed. With luck, the omission of the Moffet measles would be repaired.

"I know how pleased you will be to meet with Lady Catherine again," Clara prodded. "I am certain you will wish to fix her interest soon, Ranceford. It is time you recalled your duty to the family and set up your nursery. You must have an heir."

"I have one. Some sort of cousin some place."

Clara shrugged off all distant relations. "I mean a *real* heir. The title must be perpetuated by our immediate family."

Why? he asked, but silently. What earthly good to anyone were the Marquises of Ranceford? Dull, dull, all of them. Not an adventurer in the lot. They could use some new blood. David might have been an improvement . . .

Lady Clara was studying him, her eyes narrowed. "A family of your own, Ranceford. That's what you need. A wife and children with whom to settle down."

Settle down? What else had he done? *Until now.* He shivered, feeling the secret thrill of acting Conrad the Corsair and riding his Pacha. Little did Clara know— and for a brief time, he almost had forgot it himself. Life, all at once, became liveable again.

"Lady Catherine will make you an ideal marchioness," said Clara.

To the devil with Lady Catherine, said Conrad the Corsair, but to himself.

JULIANA SAT in her window-seat, toying with her needlework and thinking over her conversation last night with the masked man. He had made a slip and she seized on the pertinent word: Astley's. He said, before he tried to cover his faux pas, that he could not come tonight because he had to be at the Amphitheatre. Then it was vital that she be there, too.

Sir Agramont, appealed to, refused to take her, pleading a previous, and no doubt expensive, engagement with a party of friends. But, by a veritable stroke of good fortune, Percival Woffington Netherfield chose that day to pay a formal call. Juliana had no difficulty whatsoever in cadging the desired invitation from him.

Her father, as she knew he would, saw the outing as a softening of her attitude towards the despised Percy and gave instant approval.

"Certainly, certainly, my dear. I know Percy will take the greatest care of you. I stipulate only that your abigail must accompany you as chaperon."

"Naturally," said Percy, ever conscious of the strict tenets of the ton. "It would not be thought at all the thing were I to appear in so public a place with my would-be betrothed unless she were chaperoned by a responsible female."

Juliana, about to refute his claim on her as his future wife, succumbed to a fit of the giggles. Emily Jane, responsible?

"I do not see any humour in the situation, Miss Beveridge." Percy turned to her, frankly puzzled. "It is fitting that your woman attend the affair to lend you countenance in the eyes of polite Society."

Juliana managed to regain a sober expression. "Oh, it was not that. You must know, it is only that I am so pleased to be able to go with you to the Grand Equestrian Exhibition."

This satisfied Percy, who could quite comprehend a female being so desirous to be seen in his company. Of course she would be unable to contain her pleasure at the prospect.

Juliana's pleasure was naught compared to Emily Jane's, when informed of the treat in store. Wideeyed, too ecstatic to even breath "Coo!", she sank down on Juliana's dressing-table stool. She bounced up again when she realized what she'd done and began to squeal.

"Do try for more dignity, Emily Jane. Remember, you are to be a responsible chaperon." But Juliana felt her own excitement grow. Would he be there? Would she recognize him without his mask? She'd never seen him except in the moonlight. She only knew his height, his broad shoulders, his sudden smiles, the feel of his strong arms... his gentle lips....

The hours crawled like snails until she at last entered the box Percy had reserved for the evening. Eagerly, she hurried to the railing and stared about the enormous room. Her heart sank. She'd never locate him among the shouting, milling throng which filled the pit at the far end of the one-hundred-and-thirty-foot stage. But he was a gentleman; if he *was* here, he'd not be in the cheap seats below, he'd be in one of the boxes which rose in three deep tiers. They reached the domed ceiling, which had been painted with clouds and blue sky to give the impression of being out of doors, as if any outside stage could equal the opulence of the red paint, gold leaf, and green velvet curtains of Astley's Amphitheatre.

She began with as much as she could see of the bottom, less expensive, row and scanned the crowd with a deepening dismay. Hundreds and hundreds of people! And the rear of the boxes so dark and shadowy, even with the blazing light from the gigantic glass chandelier, with its fifty or more patent lamps. Sixteen smaller chandeliers, each with six wax-lights, were set against the balcony railing of the third tier up from the dirt floor, better illuminating the second row, which contained Percy's box. She took a chair by the rail and started on the boxes nearby, studying the occupants. None moved in a familiar manner, with the elegant grace she knew so well.

Percy retired to greet a friend who had waved to him. Emily Jane, for once struck dumb by the magnificence of the occasion, crouched in a seat beside her, shivering in rapture. Juliana turned her attention to the opening between the stalls where the horses and riders would make their entrance. Oh dear, suppose her masked man was one of the performers? That would explain his costume. Or perhaps he'd wear another with a different mask! Still, if he were to appear on that great stage and declaim one line, she'd recognize his voice. If she could hear it. The roar of the crowd below was deafening, and from the box next door came shrill voices, giggles and squeals.

Three girls, all acting very young and silly, hung over the balcony railing, encouraging a small boy who was chewing bits of paper into sticky wads and throwing them into the seats below. Truly, even Emily Jane displayed more decorum! Were they not under someone's control?

Leaning out over the rail as far as she dared, Juliana peered round the ornate pillar dividing the boxes—and looked straight into the eyes of the Marquis of Ranceford.

CHAPTER SIX

RANCEFORD WITHDREW HIS GAZE from Juliana's with an abruptness which bordered on insult. She gasped. Surely, he had recognized her! She knew him at once, for he had not worn a mask as Henry VIII at the ball. He need not have concerned himself! She had little or no interest in the starched-up marquis and even less in renewing his acquaintance.

Chafing from the cut direct, Juliana apostrophized the haughty marquis as a detestable, mackerel-backed, purse-proud creature, and felt a bit better. The man was so set up in his own conceit that he displayed a want of conduct quite beyond the pale. She might not be a peeress, full of juice and impeccably bred, but she was not below a show of common courtesy. Well, he'd not have a second chance!

She had meant to give the occupants of the box a disapproving glare, so she did so. Why did the man make no attempt to curb those obstreperous children? Her searching glance took in the other members of his party: an overdressed matron, no doubt the mother of the noisy brood, and a prim-faced younger woman who appeared very conscious of her consequence, every inch a member of the highest circle of Polite Society.

Juliana wondered who she was and if she were the betrothed of the stuffy marquis. An ideal *parti* for the high-in-the-instep gentleman, she decided, a female as puffed up in her own conceit as was he in his.

She considered the marquis, now seated as though frozen, with his stiff back to her. Granted, the man was handsome in a dark, romantic sort of way, but he looked to have the personality of a boiled codfish. Even Percy, though he had no sense of humour, was better company than the Marquis of Ranceford seemed to be to his party.

Percy returned at that moment, bearing glasses of light wine, including one for Emily Jane, and Juliana forgave him his faults. He was kind and thoughtful. She sat down again, accepting the wine, and lost all interest in the supercilious Marquis of Ranceford as she continued her search for her masked man.

THE FROZEN MARQUIS had every right to be petrified. What dire fate had placed Miss Juliana Beveridge in the box next to his? Had she recognized him? For a moment, she'd appeared fully as startled as he. He turned away quickly, feeling perspiration break out on his forehead.

She hadn't spoken. That was probably a good sign, from what he knew of her. Surely, if she had recognized him, she would have accused him on the spot. He'd find out soon enough, for he was meeting her tomorrow night. And he didn't mean to report a failure if he could avoid it. He'd give her those confounded vowels and get out of her life while he could still command his own.

Suddenly, he couldn't bear it any longer; he had to know if his cat were out of the bag. Clara and Lady Catherine were immersed in gossip, and the girls highly entertained by that dratted little insect, Hubert. The young cawker had his uses after all. Rance slipped from his seat and went out into the corridor behind the boxes. A few steps, and he was at the curtains backing the stalls where she sat. Opening a bare crack, he peeked in.

Miss Beveridge sat quietly, sipping from a glass and studying the people in the audience, calm-faced. She gave no sign of having made a momentous discovery and, indeed, seemed far more curious about the others in her surroundings. Percival Woffington Netherfield hovered at her shoulder, bending to pass a remark to which she made a smiling reply. Rance closed the curtain, telling himself firmly he must be pleased to see her with Mr. Netherfield. A safe choice, serious enough to curb her eccentricities. A steady, no-nonsense man. But how she would be wasted on such a bobbing-block!

Somewhat reassured as to his own safety, he returned to his box. He had not been missed. He seated himself in the shadows at the back, just in case she looked in again. A vision sprang into his mind of that piquant face peering round the pillar. How like her to be so curious as to her neighbours. And how unlike she was to Lady Catherine. He considered that lady thoughtfully as she returned polite and dignified replies to Clara's jovial remarks. Lady Catherine was a gentlewoman to her fingertips, truly the daughter of a hundred earls. Where had he heard that phrase? There hadn't been a hundred earls, but to look at Lady Catherine one could believe it. How insufferably dull to be her spouse...

HE WAS inordinately pleased, next morning, to learn that Augusta and Ophelia had joined Ethelinda and Mirabella in the nursery sick-room, and Rosamund was expected to follow. Could the Moffet measles be far behind? Nearly of a cheerful frame of mind by evening, he went on a hunt through the clubs of Saint James's for Henry Pontleby, determined to make one last try before his meeting with Miss Beveridge.

The hunt was a short one. He knew the man was a member of Brooks's, and he ran him to earth in the Great Subscription Room. Rance stood at the threshold of the long, narrow room with its green painted walls and single glass chandelier hanging from the twenty-five-foot ceiling. The four huge, round gaming tables which ran down one side were covered with green baize and lighted by tall, shaded candle stands which threw the players' faces into odd relief. Rance squinted slightly as he peered through the gloom. Not among the quinze or macao players... There, he spotted the man, seated on the opposite side of the room on one of the two red damask sofas which flanked the white-manteled hearth. A hand of cards still lay spread on the square table before him as though a game of picquet had just ended. Twin tapers cast his features in an appropriately satanic mould.

Ranceford greeted him, leaning his hands on the back of the recently vacated chair facing Pontleby. "I see you play picquet this evening. Will you not give me a game, staking Beveridge's vowels against thrice their worth?"

With a derisive smile, Pontleby scooped the cards together into a pack. "Is it not a shame," he said, a purr in his voice. "I am finished with the pasteboards for this evening. I fear they hold no appeal for me. Throwing the ivories is my game."

"Then let us cast lots."

Pontleby shook his head. "Those vowels are mine, my lord. I'll not hazard them at chance." He rose slowly, with a smile which might have charmed a lady snake, but had the opposite effect on the Marquis of Ranceford. "You are joining me Friday evening, are you not? I'll play picquet then, for any stakes you choose—except the ones you want." He clapped Rance on the shoulder. "Give over, man. The Town is full of far gamer pullets." Shoving the cards into his pocket, he strode past Rance and out of the room.

Ranceford clenched his teeth on words which fought to be uttered. Pontleby would pay dearly for that last remark. Once he got his hands on those condemned vowels, he'd beat the man senseless and let Pacha dance on the remains.

Meanwhile, there was nothing he could do but go home, change into his Corsair costume, and retrieve his horse from the Nag's Head Inn. Tonight, he'd have to report to his damsel in distress that he'd not yet slain her dragon. But when he went to Pontleby's house Friday evening, some way, somehow, he'd discover the whereabouts of those vowels and separate them from that slimy reptile.

JULIANA HEARD the hoofbeats of his horse and was on her feet, running through the dark garden to meet him. He swung from the saddle, looping the reins over one arm. As he came towards her, she threw herself on his chest, and his free arm went about her shoulders.

"Is all well?" she asked breathlessly. "Do you have the vowels?"

He was having a bit of difficulty maintaining his embrace and still holding his skittish mount. "There, there," he said soothingly. "Whoa, now. Calm down."

Juliana wasn't sure if he spoke to her or the horse, but as long as one of his arms stayed about her, she did not care. But he hadn't answered her question.

"Did you get them? Tell me!"

"Er—no. That is, not as yet. But do not worry," he added as she drew back. "I have laid a plan which cannot fail."

She studied what she could see of his face in the moonlight. The mouth beneath the black mask was set in a determined line. "What have you planned?"

He set her aside and turned his attention to hitching the horse to the leg of the statue of Prometheus he had used before. He seemed almost to be deliberately delaying his reply.

"What have you done so far?" she demanded. "Have you done *anything?*"

"Certainly, I have." He sounded wounded. "There has been a temporary failure, I admit, but—"

"You must kidnap him and take the vowels by force! With your sword—or—or a pistol."

"Good God, I could not do such a thing!"

Her nerves frayed by disappointment in her masked man, first at Astley's and now here, Juliana felt the pricking of tears. Furious at herself, she railed at him. "One-eye Willyum would better serve me! Oh, why do you not take off that silly mask?"

"What—and be recognized? Never!"

"What difference would that make? You are not much of a Corsair! Why do you not stop this nonsensical play-acting? Go! You will never rescue me!"

She pushed him away and ran back through the garden, cheating herself of the kiss she had meant to let him steal. It was over. He had failed her and she would not be such a fool again.

She would have to wed Percy and use his marriage settlement to pay off Pontleby. She told herself it wouldn't be so dreadful. Percy would make a kind and generous husband, though a dull one. She would do it and all would be well. Then why were her eyes still filling with tears as she silently swore farewell to that useless man in the silly mask?

Botheration! Was she about to make a cake of herself over a ridiculous, Gothic romantic hero who never accomplished a single rescue?

THE MARQUIS OF RANCEFORD, damaged in both pride and honour, determined to get those confounded vowels. It became vital that he show that dratted girl if he was to live with himself. He turned in at the Nag's Head stableyard, and found Willyum waiting up for him in Pacha's stall. Just the man he wanted to see.

"Willyum," he began at once, "I need some advice."

"Ah," said Willy. "I knowed yer was 'eadin' inter some kind o'rumtiddle when I seen my 'orse were gorn."

His horse! Rance let this pass. He had a matter of more urgency to pursue.

"Willyum, what should I do if someone has in his possession an item of no small value upon which I need to lay my hands?"

Willy scrubbed a chin which badly needed shaving, with a fist that could use a bit of washing—perhaps with carbolic soap. He looked the marquis up and down thoughtfully.

"You'm Quality, me lord. This 'ere'll take a might o' cogertatin'."

"Quality be damned," said Ranceford. "I'm desperate."

Willy frowned, worried. "Yer ain't thinkin' o' priggin' the kip? Yer'd get lagged, sure fire."

"If that means stealing the papers, it has already been suggested to me. Also that I try kidnapping or seizing them at pistol point."

Shock replaced the worried frown. "Yer wouldn't never, me lord!"

Rance gave the little hedge-bird a rueful grin. "No, not after witnessing your attempt in that line. However, it begins to seem as if I must use some underhanded means."

"And yer come to me fer advice." Willy nodded his head. "This 'ere ain't yer turf, me lord. Best open yer budget and lemme toss it about in me noggin. Maybe I'll 'it on summat."

Which was what he'd unconsciously hoped, Rance realized. Perhaps Willy's nefarious mind would come up with a plan. He seated himself on the edge of a water trough and, recounting a slightly expurgated version, began the tale of Sir Agramont Beveridge's gaming losses and Pontleby's demand of the hand in marriage of the baronet's daughter in payment.

Willy let out his breath in a hiss. "A right ramshackle skirter. One as deserves wot 'e'll get. The Quality fer yer, that is. Yer don't find loose fish o' that cut among our coves. Leastways, we 'as our honour, we 'as," he added, his features a mask of self-righteousness. "I'll 'elp yer, don't yer fear. Gi'me a day ter think on't. Leave all ter me."

And this Rance felt forced to do.

ONE-EYE WILLYUM proved as good as his word, though the entire next day passed with no word from him. Then, as Rance left Brooks's in the early hours of the coming morning, he was startled by a footpad emerging from the shadows before him. He relaxed when he recognized Willy.

"What the devil are you doing here?"

"Lay yer bristles, me lord. I come ter cast me glims on our villyun so's I'll know 'oo we're arter. 'E inside there?"

"Keep your voice down! Yes, standing in the doorway talking. The tall one."

As he spoke, Pontleby made a farewell gesture to the other man, who turned back and closed the door to the club. Pontleby then ambled unsteadily down the two steps to the street.

"That there is 'im, me lord? Mor'n half-sprung, i'n't 'e?"

Rance shushed him as Pontleby paused, wavering slightly, before suddenly turning in their direction.

Willy yanked the marquis back into the shadows. "'Ere 'e comes, me lord, spang into our 'ands. We'll get them papers afore the cat can lick 'er ear."

Rance eyed him with dark foreboding. "See here, what are you planning to do?"

"Why, I'm thinkin' we'd best lump is jolly nob fer 'im and mace the Joskin."

"I beg your pardon?"

Pontleby stepped from the pool of light thrown by the flambeau outside the club door. Then, before Rance could catch Willy's coattails—or rather the tails of what had once been his own hunting coat—the little road agent caught up a half brick from the gutter.

A moment later, Pontleby lay quietly in the street.

"Confound it, what the devil have you done, you scapegallows?" Rance yelled at Willyum, blenching with consternation.

Willy already knelt by the fallen Pontleby. "'Ere now, me lord. Quit yer bellerin' and 'elp me frisk 'is pockets while 'e's dreamin'."

"Demme if I ever knew such a fellow!" Rance muttered. But opportunity had knocked. He needed no further urging.

They both searched the man's garments, but to no avail. Finally, they were forced to conclude that Pontleby didn't carry the vowels on his person. Their victim began to groan.

"He's coming to." Rance hastily rebuttoned the waistcoat he'd undone. "Confound it, get out of here, Willyum!"

Silently, Willy melted into the shadows. As Pontleby struggled to rise, Ranceford helped him to his feet.

"Are you all right, man?"

Pontleby blinked his eyes into focus. "What—what happened?"

"A—ah, footpad, I presume." Rance brushed at the man's soiled coat. "I saw him attack you," he explained truthfully. "He ran when I shouted at him."

"Good God." Pontleby ran a hand through his hair, gingerly touching a rising goose-egg. "I have to thank you, my lord. You may have saved my life."

"Your purse merely, I imagine," said Rance, who had his suspicions of One-eye Willyum.

Pontleby tottered towards the club door. "Brandy. That'll revive me. Come in and I'll stand you one!" He stopped in his tracks. "I'm devilish grateful, mind you, Ranceford, but if you think I'm so grateful that I'll sell you old Beveridge's vowels, you're dead wrong."

"In that case," said the marquis, "I'll pass on your offer of a brandy for now." He steered Pontleby up the steps and back inside.

As he turned down into the street once more, Willyum materialized out of the shadows, picking his teeth.

"Been cudgellin' me brain, cully," he remarked. "Reckon we'uns 'ave to mill 'is ken."

"What?"

"Break into 'is digs. Rob 'is 'ouse."

Housebreaking! Rance stared at him, horrified. How had he got involved in such a bumblebroth. He nearly wished that dratted girl and her vowels to the devil, but there was something about her—her spirit...her independence...her warmth...the way she'd returned his kisses.... *Oh, hell and damnation.*

"How does one mill a ken?" he asked, resigning himself to a possible noose on Tyburn Hill.

One-eye Willyum scratched his flat chest pensively. "Not but wot millin' kens ain't rightly me proper lay. Howsomever, they's ways and ways, and I misdoubts we'll run into much pother. I'll think us a plan." He faded away into the shadows once more.

Rance stood on the dark street alone, silently cursing his foolishness. He should have had a premonition at the start, when Miss Beveridge hit Willy over the head and left him to cope with the corpse. Trouble, nothing but trouble, ever since he'd met that blasted girl.

THE BLASTED GIRL had troubles of her own the following evening.

Juliana and Sir Agramont were attending a dinner and informal dance at the home of one of her father's friends. Henry Pontleby claimed her hand for the first country dance. The man was far too familiar and possessive, and she tried curtly to dismiss him.

"You must excuse me, I beg you, sir. I do not wish to stand up with you."

His smile sent a cold chill up her spine. "Only two weeks left, my lovely, and you'll no longer have the right to refuse me...anything."

She drew herself up, hoping her sudden terror well hid. "You are in error, sir," she said, her voice nearly as calm as she wished. "You will be repaid in full before this month is out...somehow."

His smile tightened. "If you are thinking wedding Netherfield will free you, it is you who are in error. You belong to me. You'll come, or your father goes to prison for debt."

"Never!" she cried, like a true Gothic heroine. "I will not marry you, ever!"

Pontleby's smile became a sneer. "Have I mentioned marriage? I assure you, I have no such intention. What I offer is quite different."

A *carte blanche!* Juliana felt the blood drain from her cheeks. After a frozen moment, she rallied and attempted to strike him across the face.

He caught her wrist. "I shall enjoy this." His teeth were bared in a wolflike grin. "Taming such a spitfire will add spice to my victory."

Heads were turning their way. Juliana jerked her arm from his grip and dashed from the ballroom.

Sir Agramont was playing cards in the dining salon with two of his friends when she found him. One look at her white face and he accepted her tale of a sudden sick headache. He called for John Coachman and took her home.

In no way could Juliana bring herself to tell her father about the scene with Pontleby. For one thing, Sir Agramont would feel called upon to challenge the man and he was no swordsman, nor could he hit the proverbial barn door with a pistol.

There was but one thing to do. Send a frantic message to the masked man through One-eye Willyum at the Nag's Head by way of Emily Jane and the already suspicious John Coachman.

This time she signed it "Adorinda."

CHAPTER SEVEN

SIR AGRAMONT had been unusually quiet as John Coachman drove them home the night before. Juliana, huddled against the faded squabs in her corner, consumed by the blue devils, had not noticed his silence.

Neither of them slept well that night.

At an unusually early hour for her father, Juliana received a visit from him the next morning. She hastily hid the note to Conrad the Corsair which still lay on her desk, pushing it beneath the blotter.

He came over to her and bent to kiss her on the forehead, another rare occurrence.

"Papa, what is it?"

His manner was apologetic, and indeed he seemed almost near tears. "Ah, about Percy, my love. You may forget about marrying him."

"With pleasure."

He picked up her quill and fiddled with it, moved her sand box and finally upset her ink pot. Knowing him well, she was prepared, and caught it before her desk became a black lake.

"Don't hide your teeth with me, Papa. Out with it. What calamity faces us now?"

He looked at her, all round-eyed innocence. "Not a calamity, puss. Depending on how one looks at it. The thing is, I have been obliged to arrange another marriage for you."

Juliana dropped the quill she had taken from him. "What!"

"I had a few words with Henry Pontleby last night, my dear." Wandering over to the window, he twiddled the knob on the curtain cord. "The thing is, he refuses to give me more time to raise the funds. In fact, he said there is only one way he will give up my vowels. He wants you."

Juliana's heart, already at bottom, found it could sink further.

Sir Agramont glanced at her quickly and away again. "I am afraid you must wed him or it is ruination for us."

She could not tell him of Pontleby's proposition. When she sat silent, staring blankly into space, he backed away and slid out the door, no doubt to ease his conscience at Boodle's or White's. As soon as he was gone, Juliana pulled her note out from under the blotter and went in search of John Coachman.

Emily Jane insisted on going along to the Nag's Head. The low tavern held a strange fascination for her—as it did for herself, Juliana admitted. She longed to make one of the party. Instead, she sat in her bedchamber window-seat watching the traffic in the street below, until at last she saw their carriage come back and turn into the Beveridge House mews. Then she continued to sit for what seemed hours before Emily Jane came up to her room.

She bounded out of the window-seat. "Where were you?" she demanded before the abigail could close the door. "Has something gone wrong? Why did you not report to me at once? Did you deliver my message?"

Emily Jane appeared to be somewhat in a daze. "Oh, yus'm, I delivered it and 'e promised ta pass it on."

Reaction resulting from her anxiety sharpened Juliana's words. "Then why didn't you come to me at once?"

Emily Jane's round eyes widened in surprise. "I was apeelin' of my apple."

"You were what?" Juliana exclaimed, highly indignant. "You *knew* I waited on tenterhooks! What on earth made you stop to eat an apple?"

"I 'ad to know." The girl shuffled her feet and blushed. "'Cause Willyum said as 'ow I'm a rare strappin' wench and I 'ave rum ogles."

Juliana didn't know whether to be shocked or pleased for her. "Emily Jane, I believe you'd better translate."

"'E means as 'ow 'e thinks I'm right pretty."

Juliana looked her over. At the moment, Emily Jane *was* pretty with her cheeks pink, her eyes bright and a sort of glow about her. But she didn't consider that an excuse.

"What," she asked, quietly ominous, "has that to do with your eating apples instead of coming straight back to me? And you've lost your *H*'s."

"I 'ad—*had*—to know," Emily Jane repeated, fetching up a brown and crumpled apple peel from one of her capacious pockets and exhibiting it like a treasure.

Juliana eyed it askance. "Why are you bringing rubbish up here?"

"Oh, miss, this ain't rubbish. This 'ere is an *O*. For One-eye. I couldn't get no *W*."

"Whatever are you talking about?"

Eagerly, Emily Jane explained. "You peels your apple all in one piece. Then you twirls the peel about your 'ead three times and throws it over your left shoulder." She flushed as red as her apple had been. "The letter it makes when it lands is the initial of your—your intended."

"Emily Jane! You can't! One-eye Willyum is a highwayman!"

"Not no more," she burst out. "'E's goin' straight. 'E's yer masked man's groom now. 'E 'ired 'im on. Cares for that big black 'orse, 'e does."

At the Nag's Head Inn? Was that, then, not only One-eye Willyum's home but also that of her masked man? If she went there herself would she see him? But he had forbidden her to do so...no wonder. Naturally he feared she would track him down and discover who he was. No. She abandoned that train of thought. Her Conrad the Corsair spoke as a cultured gentleman, not one to reside in so common a tavern. Obviously, he merely had left his horse in the former road agent's care. But why?

Emily Jane broke into her reverie. "You try it, Miss Julie," she suggested with a sly wink. "Maybe you could get a *M*."

"An *M*?"

"For Masked Man."

"Oh, fustian, Emily Jane. That is not his name." Now why did she feel a surreptitious urge to reach for the abigail's worn bit of peel?

Too late, anyway. Emily Jane tucked it carefully back into her pocket. "Wouldn't be no use," she said. "It's awful 'ard to get a *W*. *M*'s 'ud be just as 'ard."

Juliana felt her gaze drawn to that pocket and resolutely turned it elsewhere. *W*'s and *M*'s, indeed. Besides . . . "How could you tell the difference?"

"Why, I collect you decides on the letter you wants to get afore you throws. Wot's 'is name, then?"

"I haven't the slightest idea, nor do I care. It's only a silly superstition, left over from the dark ages."

"It works," Emily Jane declared, stubborn. "My Aunt Conkley got a *E*. It's not easy to get *E*'s, neither."

Juliana sniffed. "It was probably an upside-down figure three."

"Well, it wasn't then!" said Emily Jane, triumphant. "Uncle Conkley's name is Edgar."

"Proof enough for anyone." Juliana grinned. She hesitated. Why not? "All right, let me try." She held out her hand.

"Oh, you 'as to use yer own apple and you 'ave to eat the 'ole thing after, core and all, saving only the pips."

Mystified—and intrigued—Juliana couldn't help pursuing the subject. "Why not swallow the pips, too? I should think that would strengthen the spell."

"You 'as to count 'em. My old granny told me so. See, the peel gives you 'is initial, eating the apple makes 'im propose, and 'ow many pips there is, them's 'ow many babies."

This was the outside of enough. "Oh, Emily Jane, go along with you. I never heard such foolishness." She shooed the superstitious abigail out the door.

Half an hour later, she wandered down to the dining-room, where a bowl of fruit usually rested on the sideboard.

There was an apple.

And a small, sharp knife inside the bowl.

Great heavens, what was she about? With a sense of shock, she realized that she'd been wondering if she would get a *C*—a *C* for Conrad. The whole idea was a piece of insanity! She could not think of the masked man in that way! Someone who might live in a tavern! If she were to save her father, her intended had best have a fortune, and a large one. Suppose she tried Emily Jane's apple-peel spell—and suppose she threw a *P*? A *P* for Percy—or Pontleby? She shuddered and ran back up to her room, leaving the apple where it lay.

At this moment, she admitted, she wanted the masked man himself, not his initial. She wanted to lose herself again in his safe, strong arms, and escape to unreality with a dashing hero who would sweep her away into his fairy tale. If only her Conrad could carry her off into a romantic novel where the heroine's horrendous tribulations were only words, the trials of the real world non-existent, and the happy ending assured. If only... if only she could simply run away from everything, riding before him on that great, prancing black horse... and probably live in near poverty in inns which would make the Nag's Head seem a palace, while poor Papa languished in Fleet Street Debtors' Prison. If only, indeed.

She wondered if Emily Jane had eaten her apple, core and all, and counted the pips.

FOR THE FIRST FEW DAYS, the Marquis of Ranceford refused to take seriously Miss Juliana Beveridge's declaration that she never wanted to see him again. Of course she did. Miffed, that was all. And he couldn't blame the poor girl for becoming upset at yet another delay on his part. But he missed the meetings in her garden at the stroke of midnight. Not, of course, seeing her—and incidentally, kissing her. No, he told himself that what he missed was riding to the rescue as his alter ego, the Corsair. The sense of freedom, escape, and adventure. The black costume, the challenge of the black horse. She would no doubt forgive and call upon him again . . . but a niggling doubt began to burgeon.

Supposing she meant to marry the well-to-do Netherfield after all... It would not be wonderful if she had had second thoughts; marriages of convenience were by far the most common in Polite Society. He could see no reason why that would not solve her, as well as Sir Agramont's, difficulties. If her only objection to the man was that he was dull, why, a great many people entered into dull marriages and managed to survive. The image of Lady Catherine's haughty, emotionless features floated into his mind. His sympathies veered suddenly to Miss Beveridge.

All right, so Percival Woffington Netherfield would make a dull husband. There were compensations for her. She would have a *wealthy* dull husband. He knew next to nothing of the man, other than that he seemed a conceited, pompous bag of wind. No, come now: that was prejudice—not jealousy!—speaking. No doubt the man had his good points and would make her an excellent spouse. With a sinking sensation, he accepted the conviction that she would soon become Mrs. Netherfield, telling himself he should feel relieved.

Then, as he stood in his chambers one morning while Beasley held up his freshly brushed coat, Jobbins appeared in the door. The butler held a silver salver on which reposed a soiled square of paper, folded and sealed all round with red wax.

Rance's heart gave a lurch and began to pound. So, she never wished to see him again, eh? He reached for the missive with a shaking hand and became aware of a positive tidal wave of curiosity emanating from Jobbins. Let the man wonder! In his elation, he felt it would do the ubiquitous fellow a deal of good not to be beforehand with every detail of his master's life. Take him down a peg. Beasley stood waiting, looking down his nose at Jobbins with a smug, condescending air, enjoying his private knowledge. Rance grinned. He knew Beasley to be no marplot, and his secret was safe.

He shrugged into the coat his valet held, and smiled blandly at his butler as he tucked the note into his pocket, unopened. "That will be all, Jobbins."

A brief flicker of frustration crossed the butler's generally expressionless features. "Yes, my lord."

Rance dismissed Beasley as well and locked his door before taking out his penknife and breaking the seal. His nervous fingers tore the paper before he could get it open and spread it out. He read the few brief lines, puzzling over the signature. Adorinda? Now what role did she play? It mattered not. She needed him once more. The Corsair lived.

He felt warmly grateful to the girl for handing him a role in which his fantasy could exist in reality, not merely in his mind. He also felt an urgent need to confer with One-eye Willyum before meeting Miss Beveridge again. Willy said he'd think up a scheme and, whatever it was, he'd give it a try. All at once, housebreaking no longer seemed so dreadful a crime. Not for Conrad the Corsair. Common thieves did it all the time. It was all a matter of laying a careful plan of procedure, and the devious mind of One-eye Willyum must have come up with one by now. Calling to one of the footmen to have his curricle brought round, he prepared to descend on the Nag's Head Inn.

As he ducked his curly-brimmed beaver at the door to the gloomy, low-ceilinged tavern, heads turned, making him acutely conscious of his well-tailored coat of blue superfine, his fawn inexpressibles and gleaming Hessians. Overpowering smells of stale tobacco, sour beer, boiled cabbage, mutton, and the unwashed multitude assailed his nostrils and he nearly stumbled going down the two steps at the entrance.

There was no sign of Willyum in the public bar or among the few slovenly figures seated at the long trestle table where meals—if one could call them that—were served. He made his way to the end of the room where shutters were thrown back from an opening over a counter. Within, he could see shelves of bottles and mugs. He came up to the serving window and a ruddy-faced, grizzle-haired man whose stained and spotted waistcoat failed to meet over his paunch peered out at him. The man wiped his hands on his filthy apron, no doubt covering them with more of the accumulated grease of ages, and glowered at Rance.

His countenance cleared like the breaking of dawn, displaying a snaggle-toothed grin. He greeted the marquis with a jovial bellow. "Oiy, you'm the flash cove what 'ired on our One-eye Willyum fer groom!"

Groom? Rance let it pass. "Where might I find him?"

Apparently he'd said something amusing, for the barkeep broke into a roar of laughter, echoed by hoots from the interested bystanders who had crowded up behind the marquis, treating him to the examination due a raree from a travelling side-show.

The publican subsided into an attack of hiccoughs. He gestured towards a back door with a grandiloquent sweep of his arm which upset the tankard he had placed on the counter for Rance.

"Where 'e allus be, cully. Out the stable, abrushin' o' that there 'orse."

Mopping the spatters of ale from his breeches, Rance thanked him and hurried out of the tavern, followed by more laughter and what he suspected were vulgar remarks.

He saw the black horse at once, tethered in front of the stable, its coat shining like satin. As Willy rose to his feet from where he'd been polishing one of Pacha's front hooves, the cantankerous beast actually nuzzled the little road agent's ear.

Willyum winked at him, touching his own forelock as an afterthought. "I thinked as 'ow yer'd be acomin' 'otfoot afore long," he said smugly.

Rance stood back, admiring the sleek horse. "I collect you've worked with horses at some time. Before you took to the high toby?"

"Aye." Willy nodded his head, startling Pacha, who still snuffled in his hair. He paused to soothe the skittish animal. "I 'opes ter give satisfaction."

As his groom? Rance chortled suddenly, imagining the expression on the face of Haskins, his head groom, should this compatriot be taken on. But to stick to the business at hand, "Be that as it may, Willyum," he said, "have you given any thought to the, er, matter we discussed?"

Willy registered hurt feelings. "'Course I 'ave. I been workin' on it. Got it all sewed up, right and tight."

Rance felt his spirits lift—and waver. "What do you have in mind?" he asked, remembering with growing trepidation Pontleby and the half brick.

"As I sees it, yer 'avter glim where 'e keeps them vowels and nip in and prig 'em. Seems like we'd best play at darkmans budge."

"And what game is that?" Rance asked, mystified.

"Why, 'at's where one o' us 'ides inside 'is ken and when alls asleepin', 'e let's t'other in."

"I see. Which of us will manage to hide inside?"

Willy grinned. "Me, o'course."

"And how do you plan to get in?"

"'At's fer me ter know and—"

"Willyum!"

"I got me a way," said Willy hurriedly. "See, I scouts the place and I meets a blowen wot works in the kitchen—" He winked broadly. "I'm sayin' no more, but now they knows me belowstairs and I knows the way in. Just gi' me the word when yer ready.''

Willy refused to explain further, grinning and looking sly when Rance pressed him. He changed the subject, in a fashion, though his mind still dwelt on the female gender.

"Speakin' o' petticoats, that there abigail o' yer gentry mort—"

"She is *not* mine."

"—Is a right bangin' chick-a-biddy."

Rance frowned. "Hold it there, Willyum. I'll not have you trying any havycavy business with Miss Beveridge's maid. Strictly off limits."

"Umm," said Willy, noncommittal. He patted Pacha's rump and the horse shied sideways, giving him an excuse to turn away. "Mebbe," he mumbled, "me intentions be honourable."

With that, Rance had to be satisfied. At least he had progress to report at the midnight meeting in the Beveridge garden.

He left his curricle and pair at the Nag's Head in Willy's charge and walked to White's for lunch, feeling a need to think and settle his nerves now that he had determined to become a—what had Willyum called it?—a ken miller. Somehow it didn't sound as bad as a thief. But what great catastrophe had occurred to make his distressed damsel call him back so urgently? Could her plans to wed Netherfield have fallen through? He hoped that was the case, for he was resolved to retrieve those damned vowels. He owed it to himself—and to Conrad the Corsair—to prove he could be a hero.

Early that evening, he returned home to an unusual silence in his house. Lady Clara met him in the hall, with a long face.

"It is just as I feared, Ranceford. Rosamund, too, has come out in the rash and is immured in her room with the shades drawn, feeling quite out of frame. I do hope," she added in her most pious tones, "that dear little Hubert has had the measles."

Rance hoped silently that Lady Catherine had not.

"Ethelinda and Mirabella are much improved, though still highly spotted," Clara went on more cheerfully. "They want their Uncle Rance to play at cards with them, for they have quite tired of Miss Blimpton. She has no aptitude for games. Ethelinda says Blimpy always loses no matter what they play and they win too easily."

"Miss Blimpton knows her place too well."

Lady Clara ignored his remark and rattled on. Rance mentally turned her off, as was his practice, and handed his hat and gloves to Jobbins, who hovered in the background. To his surprise, he missed the feeling of something happening, something going on, which usually disrupted the peace of his home. Between Augusta at the pianoforte and Rosamund with her harp, quiet of an evening was a rarity. Especially now, these desirable instruments being taken, the eleven-year-old Ophelia had elected to have singing lessons. However, he had nothing against Ethelinda and Mirabella as yet, and he could see the boredom of being shut in. He gave in with good grace and interrupted Clara's cataloguing of the elder girls' symptoms.

"Tell Miss Blimpton I'll be up to relieve her as soon as I've changed."

It would not be too bad a way to pass the time until midnight. The children were sometimes an annoyance, but in the past five years since he'd had their charge, he admitted to a warm, proprietary feeling towards them all—excepting possibly Ophelia at times.... Good God, he felt *fatherly!*

Was that so terrible? He stood in *locus parenti,* in David's shoes there, as well as in the title. Having a family of his own might not be at all bad. Always providing he didn't have a wife such as Clara. Or Lady Catherine. Now why did Miss Juliana Beveridge suddenly come to mind? That female brought only trouble! And a sense of excitement . . . of adventure . . . of being alive . . . and needed. . . .

JULIANA WAITED ANXIOUSLY at the foot of the garden that night. Had the masked man got her message? How dependable could a courier be who bore the deplorable cognomen of One-eye Willyum? If only she knew her Corsair's name and could send for him directly. She nearly giggled. She should have peeled that apple, then at least she might have known his first initial. An infinitesimal clue. Another thought: if he did come to her, what was she to tell him? She shrank from disclosing Pontleby's humiliating proposition to one who was virtually a stranger.

Minutes later, the black horse pranced into the garden, and she waited only for the man to tether it to the statue before throwing herself into the arms of that virtual stranger. She buried her face in the ruffles of his black shirt and let the warmth and comfort of his strong arms envelop her in a semblance of peace. But how could she begin? What should she say? She couldn't demand that he challenge her villain to a duel or hold him up at pistol point as she had last suggested. This was reality she faced, not a cloud of fantasy. But he was here. He had come.

She raised her head. "You received my message. I was so afraid you might not."

"Certainly. I recognized your handiwork in the sealing of the note and didn't doubt for a moment that it came from you, though I was puzzled by the signature. Why Adorinda? By the way, I like it. It suits you."

Juliana pulled away. "Good heavens, I sincerely hope not!"

"Why? It is a lovely name. Tell me about it."

In her relief at finding a safe opening topic, she began to babble and found it difficult to stop until she had related the tale of that sadly beset Gothic heroine.

"And Henry Pontleby is my Count Valnescue," she finished. "As long as he holds those vowels, I am powerless to deny him."

The masked man shook his head. "Not in this day and age."

"He—he says he will not accept money in payment for Papa's debt, so it will do me no good to marry Percy Netherfield. Pontleby wants *me*. I cannot fathom why."

"Because you've turned him down, of course," Rance said reasonably. "Some men cannot countenance defeat in any form."

He found himself staring down at her. She was lovely in the moonlight, her eyes wide with worry, her lips trembling. Her self-reliance had vanished for the moment and he suddenly felt protective, as he hadn't before. She blinked rapidly and a tear glinted on her cheek. He touched it with a gentle hand which lingered, turning her face up. His lips brushed her forehead lightly and he drew her back into his arms, hardening them about her to create a warm circle of safety, and resting his chin on her soft curls. Was that a sob he heard?

Her shoulders shook. She straightened them and gulped, glancing away. "I am *not* a watering pot. It is just that you make me feel I may give way to my deepest feelings, and I am not happy."

Right at that moment, what Rance wanted most in the world was to *make* her happy. And there was a simple solution, but one which meant a sacrifice on his part—the demise of Conrad the Corsair, or anyway his portion of that adventurer. He would have to come out in the open and drop his fantasy of rescuing his damsel by an act of derring-do which would place the vowels in her hands and himself in the role of a hero.

Since Pontleby refused to sell or game for the confounded vowels, he had only to give the needed blunt to her father. He could then see to it that it was known throughout the ton that Sir Agramont had the wherewithal and wanted to pay his debt honourably. Pontleby would have to accept it, or be known for the damnable bounder he was.

Even as he was about to speak, he perceived a hitch. If he read Pontleby's character correctly, and he was sure he did, an outright gift of thousands of pounds to a man he hardly knew would bring about the ruination of that man's daughter. Pontleby would believe he had bought the girl from her father and, in revenge, would lose no time in spreading the story abroad.

She sighed, cuddling closer. "Oh, I wish I could stay here forever," she whispered. "And let all the world go by."

Rance realized suddenly that he was wishing the same. And, good God, why not indeed? He had to marry someone—anyone but Lady Catherine—and by wedding Sir Agramont's daughter he could avert any scandal Pontleby attempted to raise. All at once, he knew he would like nothing better. Clara wouldn't care for it, but she could move to the dower house and take her undisciplined brood with her.

He had no experience in begging for a lady's hand. "Marry me, Adorinda," he said bluntly.

CHAPTER EIGHT

"MARRY ME," Rance repeated.

Juliana stared at him in shock and then began to laugh. "What?"

"I should think we would deal quite well," he said seriously.

Her laughter died. She reached up a hand and touched his cheek, just where the black mask ended. "Do you know," she said slowly, "I almost could, were I otherwise free. But marrying you would serve no purpose."

Was there a wistful note in her voice? There was an eager one in his. "Once you are wed to another, Pontleby would have to give up his ambitions."

"Sir, you are too kind, but I cannot. He would still find a way to ruin my father, if only for revenge." She gave a tiny, nervous giggle. "Do not think I haven't dreamed of running away with my noble hero and escaping into a Gothic novel where my happy ending would be assured."

Rance's heart stopped for a second, then gave an uneven bound. "What stands in your way?" he asked, his words ragged.

She shook her head. "I have no choice. I am slated to marry a fortune, Pontleby or no. Papa is quite run off his legs—to use his expression," she added hastily.

Within Ame's ace of tearing off his mask on the spot, Rance thought better of it. How different—and eminently pleasurable—to be wanted for himself and not for the wealth and title of the Marquis of Ranceford! However, it would be Lord Ranceford and not a masked corsair who paid a formal call on Sir Agramont Beveridge one morning and requested the honour of his daughter's hand. But he had his pride. First he intended to prove himself the hero she desired and get those vowels, though the devil himself opposed him.

Meanwhile, he pulled her into his arms and demonstrated what she would be missing if she married Percival Woffington Netherfield.

SHAKEN TO THE DEPTHS of her being, Juliana clung to him. How could she give him up, settle for less than the glory she now felt? Was this, then, the heart-pounding ecstasy which led to Adam and Eve being evicted from the Garden of Eden? But surely, since they went together, wrapped in each other's arms, an earthly Paradise awaited them. But what was she thinking? Oh, it must be true what they said about forbidden fruit, including Emily Jane's apple. Never should she have allowed that silly superstition to plant such thoughts about her masked man into her head, when she didn't even know if she'd have thrown his initial! She tried to push him away and failed utterly, because it was the last thing she wished to do.

He rubbed his chin in the curls by her ear. "All shall be well, my girl, wait and see," he soothed.

The vision of the happy ending she longed for wavered, and she returned to reality with much the sensation of falling from a chair which wasn't there.

"No. How can it be? There is no way for my tale to end but one." She shuddered. "Pontleby."

He kissed the tip of her nose. "Don't give him another thought. All is in train."

A spark of hope flickered into life. "What can you mean?"

"Why, I shall mill his ken, of course."

"Do what?"

"I have decided to rob his house as you once suggested. He does not carry the vowels on his person."

"How can you be sure?"

"Ah—I found an occasion to search him."

Her eyes shone in the moonlight. "Oh! Did you kidnap him? Drug his wine?"

"No, no. We merely—that is," he explained uncomfortably, "Willyum and I—one of us knocked him unconscious, so that we might go through his pockets."

She caught his hand and pressed it to her cheek dramatically. "You *are* my Corsair!"

In spite of himself, Rance felt nine feet tall. He patted her on the head. "I do my best. And this time I have a plan which cannot fail."

"Tell me!"

He hadn't meant to go into detail, but in no way could he resist those beseeching eyes.

"One-eye Willyum is to work with me. He has fixed the interest of one of Pontleby's kitchen-maids, who has divulged to him the secret entrance by which they slip in and out at night to meet, er, friends. We shall wait until all are abed. He will sneak inside and let me in. I can then retrieve your father's vowels and we will away."

In his current ebullient mood, Rance foresaw no difficulty, but his distressed damsel seemed thoughtful.

"I'd best be there as well," she announced. "There is no telling what may not go wrong." She refrained from saying so, but from years of dealing with her deplorable parent, she knew all about the male potential for making mice feet of the simplest affair.

"Certainly not!" Rance put his foot down, aghast. "This is no business for a delicate female. Suppose you are seen! You must remain at home, safely in your bed, and leave all to me."

Juliana sighed and gave in. She could not interfere while he acted the romantic hero. Hero? Great heavens, she *had* become involved in a genuine Gothic plot! She wondered if she could faint if she really tried.

IT WAS IN A MOOD both triumphant and thoughtful that Rance rode back to the Nag's Head Inn to stable Pacha. But for Miss Juliana Beveridge, his dream of playing the Corsair would have died aborning at the end of the Robertshaws' masquerade, and now it was all he lived for. When had he stopped thinking of his damsel in distress as nothing but trouble? When had she become so necessary a part of his existence?

He sent a silent paean of thanksgiving towards George Gordon, sixth Baron Byron of Rochdale, for creating Conrad the Corsair and changing his entire life. He might have gone on forever, lost in his dull world, never knowing the thrill, the romance, the adventure, of an escape into fantasy. He could no longer imagine living without his Adorinda, without the anticipation which sent his blood coursing at flood tide with his every thought of her. Could he but convince her to marry him, the word "dull" would drop from his vocabulary.

Not only Clara would be furious, he thought with a guilty twinge. There was Lady Catherine as well, if that cold female ever felt any human emotions. But *she* would only miss his title and fortune; he was sure she cared nothing for him personally. Indeed, he was certain she never considered him at all except as a necessary adjunct to becoming a marchioness. She could find another adjunct, if not another marquis.

He had become so used to Pacha's peccadillos that he scarcely noticed his shying at an early morning dray and kicking at the cart-horse, for he had just realized something which brought him up short. For the past five years, ever since David had died and thrust him into the title, he had been allowing Clara to tow him along the path of least resistance. She constantly reminded him that he must marry, and had paraded an endless stream of females past him before she determined Lady Catherine to be the most suitable in every way. In every way but the one which now mattered most to him. She didn't love him. She was probably incapable of such a vulgar feeling, and he couldn't envision ever developing any affection towards her, whereas—good God, had he developed a genuine *tendre* for the most unsuitable female of whom he could conceive?

Penniless, a reprobate of a father, a mere baronet of an undistinguished family on the fringe of Society. He threw back his head and laughed aloud, catching at the reins to save himself as the startled Pacha reared. Clara would succumb to a fit of the vapours which would surpass all her previous efforts. He'd best break his momentous news at a time when the doctor was in the house attending to his nieces' measles!

He hadn't a doubt that he'd have such news. Sir Agramont Beveridge would leap at the chance to acquire the Marquis of Ranceford for a son-in-law, but Rance began to worry about Juliana's reaction. Would she prefer her masked Corsair? Though not one puffed up in his own conceit, he knew well the worth of Lord Ranceford, and therefore knew also a creeping unease. Which would she choose, him—or his title? He had to find out.

JULIANA OPENED HER EYES at dawn, her dreams fleeing on the instant, leaving only an odd sense of comfort and happiness. Now, why? Between her father and Pontleby, all her world was in chaos. Then memory returned as she came fully awake. Her Corsair had offered for her, and he had meant that offer.

Oh, she had been sorely tempted, but the very idea was impossible. Considering the situation with her father and Henry Pontleby, it would be a misalliance as ill-advised as Emily Jane's hopes of One-eye Willyum. But thinking of Emily Jane reminded her...

The house was very still. Her abigail and the Conkleys were not yet about and Sir Agramont hardly settled into his bed. Downstairs, in a bowl on the sideboard, that apple waited. Why not? It wouldn't hurt to have a try. Afterward, she could eat the apple and no one would ever know.

She ran down to the dining-room in her bare feet, returning with the apple and the silver knife. Seated on the edge of her bed, she began the surprisingly difficult task of cutting all the peel in a single piece. Emily Jane said it was not easy to get an *M*. She would try for a *C*. What, she wondered, was his real name? It might really be Conrad, but somehow that didn't seem likely.

There, her peel was finished. Juliana looked at it doubtfully. It was entirely too long to be a simple *C*;

she should have made a wider, shorter strip... but maybe she'd get his actual initial. She stood in the centre of her hearthrug, the only clear space in her small room, and twirled the peel round her head. Once, twice, three times, and over her left shoulder. Almost fearfully, she studied the result.

It certainly was not a *P*, ruling out both Percy and Pontleby. No, Pontleby would be an *H* for Henry. It was not an *H*. How silly to feel thankful! This was only a game. But what could the letter be? Not *C* or *M*. In fact, viewed from the side, it seemed to be more like an *S* than anything else. A safe letter. She knew no man among her father's acquaintance with that initial, and none among her own who were like to make her an offer, which proved it a silly superstition. Absurdly relieved, she tossed the peel out her window, and settled down to eat the apple. The core, pips and all, followed the peel down into the street.

Several hours later, she once again sat in her favourite window-seat, this time perusing volume 1 of *Adorinda* for the second time and reading with new, more sympathetic eyes. Her attention was attracted to the street below by an elegant, crested carriage pulling up at their door. She leaned out for a better look and recognized the top-lofty Marquis of Ranceford as he walked up their steps.

What on earth could he want with Papa? Dismayed, she wondered if her unlucky father had lost some vast sum to the marquis and he had come in person to collect. It would be a short visit, for his mettlesome team awaited him rather than being walked by his groom.

In barely ten minutes he came out, mounted his carriage, and was driven away. His departure was followed by the arrival of Sir Agramont at her door, panting after taking the stairs two at a time.

"Puss!" he cried. "We are saved! You'll never credit what has happened."

Juliana, frightened by the flush on his cheeks, rose quickly and pushed him into a chair. "Calm down, Papa! You'll go off in an apoplexy."

He was gasping for breath but he bounded from the chair. "We are saved!" he repeated. "I did not even know you were acquainted with him."

"Ranceford? I know him only slightly."

"My dear, you are about to know him a great deal better. Juliana, my love, my dearest girl, he has *offered* for you!"

Juliana sat down in the chair he had vacated, the blood drained from her own cheeks. "Papa, you cannot be serious."

Sir Agramont nodded so vigorously that his velvet morning cap, all he had left of his dressing attire, slid awry. He didn't notice. Pacing the floor and rubbing his hands together, he chortled with delight. "You cannot conceive the pleasure it will give me to inform Pontleby that I shall soon have the blunt to reclaim my vowels. Ranceford is making a most satisfactory marriage settlement."

"Papa, wait." Juliana tried to catch his sleeve. "I have not agreed to this. I do not wish to marry that man! Why, I have hardly spoken half a dozen words to him. There must be some mistake."

"No mistake. He asked for your hand and I gave it to him."

"No! I won't do it! Papa, you cannot force me to wed a man I—I have taken in dislike!"

Sir Agramont stopped his pacing and faced her. She drew back from a father she scarcely recognized. He spoke, quietly ominous.

"Juliana, I am out of patience with you. You have refused two respectable offers, first Netherfield, then Pontleby. This one you will not turn down. You cannot be so addlepated as to whistle down the wind so fabulous a fortune."

Juliana began to regain her spirit and rallied. "You mean *you* do not mean to do so. You would sell me to the highest bidder like a piece of Haymarket ware!"

He shook a finger in her face. "I'll not have you speak such vulgar words in this house. My dear girl, there is no question of striking a bargain with the man. He has made a legitimate offer and I have accepted it."

"*I* have not!"

He changed his tactics. "Think, Juliana, you will be a marchioness. Go in to dine right behind a duchess. A countess must give way to you!"

"And I must give way to a cold, haughty bore!"

Sir Agramont snorted, huffy in the extreme. "I have said my last word on the matter. It is settled. I leave you to your thoughts."

"Oh, you needn't. I do not mind airing them."

"Well, I mind hearing them." Her door slammed as he left.

Juliana sank down on her bed, prey to a severe case of the dismals. Papa was adamant. This was not a match he'd give up, even had he those—those *damnable* vowels in hand. And who could fault him? He envisioned untold wealth showered upon him, an entrée to the Society of the haut ton he craved, all his dreams come true. How cruel a daughter she'd be to deny him . . . But this was *her* life he sold so joyfully, her whole *future*, and she wouldn't submit without a battle.

Sir Agramont had been carrying Lord Ranceford's calling card when he came in, and he'd dropped it on her desk. The white square caught her gaze. Almost afraid to look, she picked it up and read the engraved name: Stephen Gregory Allmont, Marquis of Ranceford. An *S* . . .

She stared at the card in horror. Was it an omen? Was this to be her fate? *No!* She stamped her foot. Truly, she was becoming as foolish as Emily Jane. And even if she married the man, it would not solve her problem. An insidious foreboding crept over her like a darkening cloud. Henry Pontleby would not give up so easily. He would find a way to ruin her, if only for revenge.

HER PREMONITION proved correct. After a nuncheon she hardly touched, she collected Emily Jane and went to Green Park in an attempt to walk off her attack of the blue devils. Pontleby was there. He made a point of crossing her path, bringing her to an unavoidable confrontation. Her devils multiplied tenfold.

Emily Jane shrank behind her, catching at her shawl. "Coo," she whispered, entirely too audible. "Iffen it ain't that Bad Man!"

"Hush!"

Pontleby's eyebrows raised. "Hush, indeed, my dear. Send her away. My words are for your ears alone."

Emily Jane moved not an inch, clinging to Juliana's arm. "I stays with my miss."

Pontleby frowned. "If you care to have your affairs common knowledge among every domestic in London, Miss Beveridge, I do not. Send her off."

"It's all right, Emily Jane." Juliana gave the abigail a gentle push. "Wait for me by that bench. This will only take a minute."

"Quite right." Pontleby watched Emily Jane's reluctant retreat. "I merely wish to remind you, my dear, that it is not money I demand. I have just so informed your father. If you know what is good for him, you had best refuse your wealthy suitor."

"My suitor!" Juliana exclaimed. Shaken in spite of her determination to stand up to him, she tried to dissemble. "I am barely acquainted with the man."

Pontleby's smile froze the words crowding into her throat. "See that you keep it that way, or I may find it necessary to drop a flea in Ranceford's ear. He'll not tolerate being taken for a flat by a debt-ridden rum touch."

Juliana turned away abruptly, head high. She walked stiffly back to Emily Jane, followed by a gloating chuckle.

Somehow, some way, her masked man had to make good!

RANCE WAS grimly determined to do just that. He would not fail Juliana this time. The evening of his appointment with Pontleby for dinner and cards had arrived, Willy was primed and their adventure ready to unfold. As keyed up as a race horse awaiting the starting gun, he ruined three neckcloths before achieving a desirable effect. Tomorrow, in the garden at midnight, the Corsair would ask Adorinda once more to marry him, and present her with Sir Agramont's cursed vowels as a betrothal gift. But would she accept him in his guise as her masked hero now that the highly eligible Marquis of Ranceford had offered for her? Somehow, that question was all-important.

Pontleby's home was one of a block of separate houses on the fringe of Town, divided from each other by tall hedgerows. Rance discovered, on arriving, that he was the only guest and wondered at the man's reason for wanting a tête-à-tête. Suspecting a nefarious purpose, he feigned innocence. With the butler standing properly by with his back to the sideboard, only small talk prevailed throughout the meal. However, once the table was cleared and they sat at their port, Pontleby turned the conversation to Sir Agramont Beveridge and the prize both wished to claim.

"I hear," he said, butter not melting in his mouth, "that you have offered for the chit."

Rance nodded. "I have indeed, and her father has accepted my offer."

"We shall see who wins that game." Pontleby tossed off the rest of his wine. "My cards are on the table, Ranceford. I intend to have her. Speaking of pasteboards, let us play—but for quite different stakes. I do not risk those vowels."

He preceded Rance into the bookroom, where a gaming table, already set up, awaited before the hearth. Seating himself, Rance remarked, as casually as he could, "I suppose you keep them in a safe place?" For a moment, he feared his query to be clumsy, but Pontleby seemed unconcerned.

"In my study," he said, gesturing at the ceiling directly above his head. "They are locked in my desk and there they stay until my negotiations are complete. Which," he added with a smirk, "I assure you they will be. You may as well accept defeat, my lord. The wench will be mine."

Already the victim of galloping nerves, Rance had expected difficulty concentrating on his play, but anger at Pontleby's derogatory attitude towards Miss

Beveridge sharpened his wits and he came off the victor when Pontleby finally called a halt.

He had had no notion why the man had invited him for so innocuous an evening, but soon found out.

"It is a beautiful night, is it not?" Pontleby asked as they rose from the table. "Let us step outside and blow a cloud before you depart."

Raising his eyebrows, Rance followed him out onto a terrace lined with French windows, one pair of which led to the room where they had just dined.

Pontleby strolled towards the corner and casually pointed at a gigantic oak tree whose limbs brushed the balcony above them.

"Many's the time," he told Rance, "that tree served as my staircase when I was a boy. It is right next to my study window."

So that was his game. Did the clodpole think he'd climb that tree and attempt to break into his study? Rance lighted a cigar with fingers he forced not to shake. "Sneaked out a bit, did you?" he asked, as though completely uninterested.

"Aye, and came home late. Which reminds me, I am about to leave Town tomorrow, to visit for a few days at the home of my earliest childhood—my estate in the country."

Rance felt quite insulted that the man would think him so stupid as to fall for so obvious a trap. His plans were for tonight, not tomorrow when Pontleby, or perhaps a footman, would wait in the dark study with a shotgun. He played along, pretending to portray a

barely concealed eagerness, and Pontleby seemed satisfied. Tonight, then, should be clear, and he had no
intention of climbing trees.

He called for his curricle and took his leave, driving only until out of sight at the end of the hedgerows. Willy materialized from the dark shadows.

"We're in luck," Rance told him. "I know where
the vowels are hidden. How are you at opening locked
desks?"

For answer, Willy winked and patted his pocket.
"Easy as Bob's yer uncle."

"I hope that's not an omen. My uncle's name is
James. Enough. Here is where we must go." Rance
explained the layout quickly. "Around to the side of
the house there is a terrace with French doors, one of
them opening to the dining-room. Hide in there. I'll
be right outside. As soon as you are sure all are abed
and quiet, let me in."

Willy nodded and signalled a thumbs up.

"And don't get caught!"

"Don't matter if I do." Willy grinned, crooked teeth
flashing in the moonlight. "They'd only think I snuck
in fer a quick slap'n'tickle w'that there scullery maid."

Rance clapped him on the back, raising a wisp of
dust. "Then luck be with you."

Willy disappeared back into the shadows in the
manner so peculiarly his own. Rance watched him go,
then unrolled his Corsair costume from under the
curricle seat and changed into it, even donning his
mask. It seemed, somehow, the proper thing to do if

he didn't mean to be recognized should their plan go awry. He settled down to wait for all light to vanish from Pontleby's windows before he approached the house. Now, if only Willy's scullion spoke truth and had told the little thief of an entrance . . .

An hour later, a candle and tinder-box in his pocket, he crouched on the terrace outside the chosen French window. His quivering nerves were on fire and he knew a tendency to jump at every falling leaf. He decided to remove his boots so he might enter on silent stockinged feet, and reached for one, wondering if Willy were safely inside. . . .

In another moment, he had no such doubts and he dived into a handy shrub. Inside the house, an eerie caterwauling filled the air, a too-familiar voice raised in jug-bitten, bawdy song.

Minutes later, the French window flew open, but not for him. Willy sailed out into the night, propelled by the large foot of a muscular butler wearing only a nightshirt, cap, and Turkish slippers with pompons on the toes.

CHAPTER NINE

THE FRENCH WINDOW slammed shut and Ranceford crawled out of the bush, picking bits of twig and leaves from his crimson-lined cape. He looked down at the recumbent One-eye Willyum, disgusted. Willy returned his scrutiny with a vacuous beam.

"Castaway!" Rance exclaimed. "Drunk as a wheelbarrow! I might have known you'd make a confounded mull of it, you dismal cawker! You mutton-witted, bacon-brained, addlepated hedge-bird!"

Willy waved a finger vaguely in the air. "You'm vexed," he pronounced.

"Oh, for God's sake, come on. We'd best take our departure before we're discovered."

He picked up the little highwayman and succeeded in setting him on his feet after a few tries. Taking him by the shoulders, he steered him towards the hedgerow where he'd hitched his team and curricle. He did a bit of lurid cursing. It was his own fault; he'd made a tactical error in suggesting Willyum wait in a dining-room where the sideboard would be topped with a row of decanters. He gave Willy an extra shove, nearly toppling him into a rhododendron.

"Now you've done it," he told him. "I daresay you won't be able to let me in again. You're a hell of a ken miller."

The fresh air had revived Willy, and he complained. "Never said I was. I'm a road agent, I am."

"You weren't much good at the high toby either, as far as I could see."

"I be willin' to learn. That were me first."

"I'm surprised they only threw you out of here. It would not have been wonderful if they'd held you and called in the watch."

"Yer fergettin' the maid," said Willy, with a fatuous smirk. "Reckon she might see 'er way ter gettin' me a spot o' work in the stable iffen yer want. Muckin' out stalls ain't no bed o' roses, but I 'ud be on the spot."

Rance boosted him up into the curricle. He unhitched his pair and climbed up on the other side.

"I don't think we can count on that. After the devilish commotion you've just raised, that butler will no doubt rouse your bit of muslin and serve her a potent word or two. You may have lost her position for her."

Willy leaned back, smoothing the leather seat. "Never rid in one o' these afore," he marvelled. "Don't you worry none about Elsie. 'Er and that butler be like April and May." His voice in the darkness purred complacently. "That'd be wuffor 'e'm so discombobulated. Jealous, that's wot."

Be that as it may, once again Rance would have to report a failure to his Adorinda. Exasperated, he set his teeth and gave his horses the office. They moved off into the night. Devil take it, now what would he do?

Willy's evening had not been a total loss, however. He'd made another assignation with the kitchen maid. And that was not all he'd gained. As Rance drove them back towards the Nag's Head, he took from one of his capacious pockets a quizzing glass with gold filigree frame and carved ebony handle. Mimicking the airs of a Bond Street Beau, he used it to survey the houses they passed. They turned into a street illuminated by the new gas lights and Rance saw what he had.

"You filched that!" he exclaimed. "That's stealing! Do you want to get us both nicked? Now we'll have to go back and break in there again to replace that glass where you found it before it's missed!"

Willy was aggrieved. "It was just alayin' there on a table. 'E couldna wanted it much like."

Rance, unaccustomed to travelling with one of the light-fingered gentry, was horrified. "It must be returned at once! Oh, hell and the devil confound it, we can't go back tonight. It will be dawn before all in that house are settled down again."

He knew a strong disinclination to return at all, but due to One-eye Willyum's sticky fingers, they had no choice. Pontleby would suspect no connection between the Marquis of Ranceford and tonight's affair. In his mind, Rance ran over the conversation on the terrace. Pontleby couldn't have meant his words the way he'd perceived them. How could the man ever imagine a peer of the realm would sink to—to ken milling? His own guilt must have imbued the scene with iniquitous undertones which had never been there.

By the time they reached the tavern, Rance had almost convinced himself he'd read far more into the interlude than existed. And they had to return that quizzing glass before it was discovered to be stolen and not merely mislaid.

He pulled the curricle to a stop at the entrance to the inn and drew a deep breath. "We must go back, Willyum. To return your ill-got gain."

Willy, who had climbed down, looked up at him, all innocence, and held up a small object. "Then I reckon yer want I should give back this 'ere enamel snuff-box as well."

Rance groaned. "What else did you pilfer?"

"Nuttin', I swears."

"Thank God for that. Only He knows how we'll get in this time. I'll be damned if I climb that blasted tree."

"Why'd yer want ter do a daft thing like that fer?"

"To get into the house, of course."

Willy grinned. "That 'ud be a treat ter see, but them kitchen maids leave a pantry window off the latch so's they can get out o' nights."

"I might have known you'd be fly on every suit."

Shaking his head, Rance drove off, leaving Willy chortling to himself in the doorway.

THE NEWS of Ranceford's visit to Sir Agramont brought a not unexpected reaction from another quarter. As Juliana sat in the morning parlour pretending to set stitches in a piece of needlework, she received a visit from Percival Woffington Netherfield. He stopped, posing dramatically just inside the door.

"I have been told by Henry Pontleby that your father has received an offer for you from Ranceford," he declared. "I have come to hear you deny it."

Juliana laid down her needle, and answered with composure. "Then I am afraid you have come in vain."

He came towards her, blustering. "You must know it is my intention to wed you! Has been these many years; I waited only for you to attain a respectable age!"

"Percy, you know I will not marry you. I have told you so innumerable times."

He forced a smile and would have caught her hands had she not quickly put them behind her.

"Now, now," he said as though humouring a backward child. "No need to continue to be missish. You have played coy quite long enough and these pretensions of Ranceford's must be discouraged immediately. You will, of course, hand him his *congé*. The time for this sportive courting between us is past."

"Percy, it never began. Please believe me. I do not mean to marry you."

An inkling of her sincerity began to percolate through the miasma of his overweening self-esteem. He hastened to set her straight. "Juliana! I am your father's heir! I shall own this house and his title. It has been understood since your birth that I am to marry you for your own provision. When Sir Agramont dies, you will be left penniless!"

The Marquis of Ranceford came suddenly into Juliana's mind. The man could be of use.

"Not," she said, smiling sweetly, "if I am the Marchioness of Ranceford."

She had actually said those fateful words aloud. The dark cloud of doom which had hovered over her head suddenly descended to sit upon her shoulders. She had intimated that she might marry the man. Her stomach cramped and she shrank into herself like a salted snail at the very thought of that cold, emotionless creature laying his hands on her person.

No! She'd suffer no one to touch her but her Corsair with his warm arms and gentle lips...holding her against his broad, solid chest...murmuring comforting phrases in his deep, soft voice...riding up to her on his prancing steed with his lovely black cape...and his empty pockets. She gave herself a mental shake. But not Percy—not Pontleby—and *not* the Marquis of Ranceford!

Percy, dumbfounded, was gawping at her like the pool fish he so frequently resembled. She turned him about and pushed him out the door.

He was replaced within minutes by another aggravation, Sir Agramont, who began speaking before he entered the room. "Juliana? Oh, Juliana, there you are. Pontleby seems to think your marriage to Ranceford will never come off. I cannot imagine what would prevent it, but all in all, I feel we'd best have you wed as soon as may be. I have just come from Ranceford and he is quite willing to make haste in the matter. We have agreed to seven days' time."

"Seven days!" The doom cloud ceased shilly-shallying on her shoulders and swarmed over her like a smothering blanket. "One week! Papa, that is not even time to post the banns!"

"It is all the time I have," he explained reasonably. "Pontleby has increased his demand for payment, and I was forced to remind him that the end of the month is still ten days away."

Juliana spun about and fled desperately for the privacy of her room before tears disgraced her.

Privacy was not to be hers.

She opened the door on a curious sight. Emily Jane, her back to Juliana, knelt on the hearthrug, her head on the floor and her other end necessarily elevated. Her face was turned towards the fire, and an inch from her nose stood one of Sir Agramont's best wineglasses filled with water.

"May I ask," Juliana demanded, "what on the green earth you are doing? Oh, do be careful!"

At the opening of the door, Emily Jane had scrambled up with a startled shriek. The wineglass went over, soaking the rug, and Juliana ran to pick it up.

"It's not broken, luckily for you," she exclaimed. "That is one of our last good set!"

"I 'ad to use a good one." Emily Jane knelt again, mopping ineffectually with her apron at the puddle which rapidly sank into the rug. "So's I'd get a real clear picture."

"Never mind the water. The fire will dry it out. Just tell me what you were doing." Juliana set the wineglass carefully on the mantel and sat down on the edge of her bed.

Emily Jane flushed and scrubbed one toe on the back of her other ankle. She didn't answer.

"I see. More divination." Juliana shook her head. "Really, Emily Jane. You can't be serious."

"This one is supposed to work," the abigail explained earnestly. "You look through water at fire and you sees the face of the one what loves you."

"And did you see a face?"

Emily Jane hung her head. "No'm. Not so's I recognized 'im."

"You won't, either. Do give over. Or at least," she added, suddenly recalling something her masked man had said about a scullery maid, "try another man. One-eye Willyum is not what I would consider an excellent choice."

"It 'as to be 'im, Miss Julie. No one else ever told me I was pretty."

Juliana bit her lip, her own troubles set aside in her concern for her abigail. Should she tell Emily Jane about Willyum and the scullery maid in Pontleby's house? Or was that only the sort of affair men thought well-bred females knew nothing about? Emily Jane might not be as well-bred as a lady of Quality, but she could be just as badly hurt. She studied the pink, eager face of her young abigail uneasily.

"He's a highwayman, Emily Jane. Bound for the gallows. You'd be a widow before you turned round."

"I told you, Miss Julie." The girl stuck out a stubborn lower lip. "'E's on the straight and narrow. 'E told me."

Not now he wasn't, Juliana thought guiltily. Not when he was involved with her masked man in breaking into a house to steal back her father's vowels. To steal . . . and it was all her fault! Her masked man . . . Her heart froze.

"Emily Jane, your Willyum may not be the only one to hang!"

THE SAME THOUGHT had occurred to Ranceford, and more than once. However, he was rapidly discovering in himself a hitherto unrecognized streak of daring which abetted his longing for adventure, though it was as yet tempered by his basic sense of caution. Nevertheless, he found himself reluctant to face Miss Beveridge with yet another tale of failure. It was so—so *lowering* to constantly confess delays.

He dined at home that evening, not being in a festive mood and feeling the need of a clear head for his midnight encounter in the garden. Lady Clara had gone out, a dinner invitation from one of her bosom bows, a woman Rance considered the worst gossipmonger in London. No doubt the reason for Clara's accepting her hospitality, for she made it her purpose in life to be *au courant* concerning the latest crim. cons.—as well as knowing it safer to be among those present at such gatherings.

Augusta, Rosamund and Ophelia having reached the whining stage of their affliction, Rance took refuge in the nursery. There he lingered over card games with Ethelinda and Mirabella—even allowing himself to win one or two to bolster his sagging ego—until Miss Blimpton fairly ordered him from the room with the announcement that it was outrageously past their bedtime.

Clara had returned from her session of scandal-broth and pounced on him as he entered the hall.

"Ranceford!" she cried, clutching her breast and gazing at him as though pleading for rescue from a turbulent sea. "Tell me! What is this tale I have heard of you and old Beveridge's daughter?"

For a moment, Rance's knees turned to the water in which she figuratively drowned, and he nearly fell to the floor in shock. An ancient and uncomfortably carved armchair stood directly behind him and he managed to collapse in it almost as though it had been his intention to sit. He crossed his elegant ankles before him and bent over, brushing non-existent dust from his impeccably gleaming boots. The respite allowed him a few seconds in which to school his features into a semblance of mild curiosity. Clara, up in the boughs, failed to notice his reaction.

"I can't imagine what you might have heard from that group of gabble-tongued, hen-witted females," Rance said, carefully containing a tendency of his voice to rise an octave.

His mind raced. Good Lord, had the very bushes— or that statue of Prometheus—sprouted operating ears? Who could have spied on their midnight meetings? Suddenly, he was terrified. What would this do to the girl's reputation? Should he confess all to Clara, and claim his Adorinda as his intended bride to squelch any scandal which might arise? Or deny everything? Prudently, he kept his tongue between his teeth until he heard more. Not that he could have squeezed a sentence of his own in edgeways, for Clara's words rolled over him like an avalanche.

"They say you have *offered* for her! And it must be the truth," she wailed, "for Lady Bostock had it directly from her maid, who is walking out with the Greenlys' second footman. He is related to the Cranstons' housekeeper, who is the aunt of Mr. Percival Woffington Netherfield's valet and who heard it direct from him! Tell me at once that it is a lie!"

Now under control, Ranceford raised marquisian eyebrows. "No such betrothal exists," he said, which so far was perfect sooth. "At least, not to my knowledge, and surely Miss Beveridge would have told me of it."

"There!" exclaimed Clara. "And did I not so inform that quiznunc right to her face! Fustian, I told her. Nonsense. Ridiculous. You must have confused the names, I said. It is well known to all the ton that you intend to offer for Lady Catherine Moffet."

"It is not well known to me." Rance felt his wrath building in direct relation to his terror of a few moments before. It was time to put an end to Clara's machinations. "And it will not be," he added firmly.

"What!" She stared at him, incredulous.

"I have decided we would not suit."

"*You* have decided! Ranceford, you are well aware—"

He rose to his feet, his knees again his own.

"Once and for all, Clara, I will not be coerced into a marriage I do not desire. In fact, I believe I will look over this Miss Beveridge, since you seem to feel her capable of fixing my interest."

She shrank from him, rather as if a placid sheep had turned and suddenly bitten her. "But—but what am I to say to Lady Catherine?"

"I fail to see why you must say anything. It is none of your affair. I have given no encouragement to her attempts to cast her handkerchief in my direction. Indeed, quite the opposite. I have not offered for her and I have no intention of doing so. If you had any such plan, I pray you disabuse yourself of it. I suggest from now on that you confer with me and ascertain my opinion on any future ideas which may find a roost in your empty cock-loft.''

Victorious, he retreated from the battlefield, heading up to his chambers. His last view of Clara showed her sitting in the chair he had vacated, gaping after him. He hoped that carved knurl in the centre of the back had stuck into her, too.

It helped for a while, but he still had to face his Adorinda with empty hands. But not for long! That packet of vowels had blossomed into a veritable holy grail in his eyes, to be retrieved at whatever cost to life and limb.

JULIANA MUST ALSO have spent the day in a fever of impatience, for she scarcely waited for him to secure Pacha to the statue of Prometheus before running into his open arms like a rabbit bolting into its burrow.

"You have not been hanged!" she cried.

Rance felt his neck with one hand, turning his head from side to side. "I do not believe so. My neck still supports my head."

In answer, she twined both arms about that endangered neck and held up her face to be kissed. The Corsair would not be one to waste such an opportunity, nor did Rance, especially since this blissful moment would soon be blasted.

He started to tell her of their thwarted attempt to steal the vowels, but she interrupted.

"The most dreadful thing has happened! Papa has arranged a perfectly repellant marriage for me!"

"Has he now?" His heart banging a triumphal march, Rance buried his face in her hair to hide a grin which bade fair to split his face ear to ear. So, the wealthy and titled Marquis of Ranceford could not compete with himself! He would win her yet—as soon as he straightened out one bosky highwayman.

"And when is this objectionable marriage to take place?" he asked, trying to sound crushed.

She looked up, her eyes tragic in the moonlight. "In one week's time, by special licence, for Pontleby demands payment in less than ten days. So you see, we must have those vowels at once. And even when he has them in his hands, Papa will still use any means to force me to marry the Marquis of Ranceford. But then, at least, I shall be able to run away without a burden of guilt."

Rance, who had not let her go, enveloped her in a closer embrace. "You do not wish to be wealthy beyond dreams of avarice?"

"Oh, no. I have never been wealthy, so how should I miss it?"

This called for another, longer kiss. Rance felt like singing, not unlike One-eye Willyum amid Pontleby's decanters. Truly, he felt quite cup-shot!

Juliana sighed as he raised his head, and she suddenly giggled. "I feel so safe here with you. It is only that I have foolishly allowed myself to be overset by Emily Jane and one of her nonsensical superstitions which had all the earmarks of an omen. It concerned an apple peeling spelling out an initial. No matter how

I threw it, it became an *S*. Then I learned Ranceford's name was Stephen, and I thought oh, I am for it!''

He gave her an odd look. "Ah—what initial were you hoping for?"

Juliana felt herself blushing furiously, and was thankful for the darkness. "Truly, I do not know," she said, and realized that betrayed her as well.

She felt, rather than heard, the chuckle deep in his chest, and pulled away, trying ineffectually to smooth her hair. "But what has been happening?" she asked. "You have not told me. You said you had devised a plan. How soon can you put it to the trial? There is not much time."

There was also no help for it. Too honest to try evasion, Rance launched into the story of the previous night's fiasco.

"Oh, why did you not let me come?" she exclaimed. "I knew something would go wrong if I were not there to help."

"You?" he demanded, somewhat nettled. "What could you have done? At least I now know where the vowels are kept. They are in a desk in Pontleby's study above his dining-room. He even expects me to try to steal them. He very politely pointed out the end of the terrace where a huge tree overhangs the small balcony outside his study window. But I am not," he added bitterly, "going to climb that tree, if that is what he had in mind."

Juliana's nerves were somewhat frayed and this seemed to her a rather cowardly approach. So close!

Those vowels were almost in his hands. Forgetting all about gallow-trees, she stamped her foot. "Why not? Are you afraid? If the vowels are there, within easy reach, why are you not at his home right now, making your way after them?"

"Because I am not a fool! When a better opportunity comes, I shall take advantage of it."

"But I need those vowels *now!* Oh, you are utterly useless as a hero!"

Rance stiffened. "In that case," he said, "perhaps I'd best retire from your service."

"Yes, you had!"

"Yes. Very well, then. I'll be on my way."

"All right, go!" Near tears, and at a loss for words suitable for a young lady of Quality, she turned her back on him.

This did not seem a good time to go down on one's knee and beg for the lady's hand. Rance bowed a formal farewell, and mounted Pacha, who was quite ready to leave. He rode off to the Nag's Head, thinking longing thoughts of strangling One-eye Willyum.

Juliana's tears burst through, and she ran back to the house where Emily Jane—also bursting, but with curiosity—waited to let her in by the side door.

CHAPTER TEN

JULIANA HAD REGRETTED her foolish words as soon as they left her lips, but it was too late. The masked man rode off before she could call them back. She lay awake until the first faint light of dawn, her mind running in circles around a growing fear. Had she sent him off determined on a reckless act? She could not let him be hanged for her! It was *her* problem, and up to her to solve it. She was no Adorinda to stand meekly by while the hero risked his life.

Now that he had discovered for her the location of the precious vowels, it was time to take matters into her own hands before her masked man met a not-to-be-thought-of end. Breaking into a house could not be all that difficult. Gentlemen, she knew, spent their evenings at their clubs, drinking and gaming until all hours. Pontleby would not be at home after dark, and that meant his servants, like the proverbial mice with their master away, should be in their own quarters and, she hoped, at play. If she could find a forgotten window and slip inside... It was worth a try, and one she'd best make at once before her masked man could act.

Her decision made, she finally slept.

THINGS NEVER LOOK the same in the morning. Juliana awoke to serious misgivings. If Pontleby did not go out this evening, she would be caught. She had no idea when he would leave his house or at what hour he might return. But Papa would know.

She ate breakfast in solitude as usual, and also her early nuncheon, but then caught Sir Agramont just as he left his bedchamber.

"Good morning, Papa," she began brightly. "Off to your clubs?" Even to her ears, her voice sounded so over-casual that she quaked with anxiety. How could he not suspect some rig was in train?

"Ah, puss." He beamed at her. "You seem more cheerful. I am glad you realize your old father knows what is best for you."

"You mean for *you*," she murmured, but to herself. "Does Mr. Pontleby frequent your same clubs?" she asked instead, in the same false tone.

"Well, of course he does. There are only just so many houses a gentlemen may visit."

And I daresay you know all those a gentleman may not, she thought. "Then you will be like to meet him tonight?"

"No, I won't. Saw him yesterday and he said he'd be out of Town for a few days. Going to his place in the country. Urgent business, he told me. No doubt planning to fleece some country squire. No, no," he interpolated hastily, as though sensing from her face that he had erred. "Only bamming you, my dear. He's an excellent fellow. Make you an unexceptionable husband should Ranceford fail." He sidled round her and made for the door.

"Good," Juliana said aloud to the now-empty hall. "Go away, Papa, so you will not know what I am about."

With Pontleby out of Town, she needed only for Sir Agramont to stay at White's, or Boodle's, or Brooks's, she cared not which, for a night of his unfortunate gaming.

But she could not carry off her scheme without an accomplice. It would not do for a lone female to walk the streets of London in the middle of the night, nor could she count on hiring a hackney. There was one person whom she could trust implicitly—and who would be sure to present every argument in the book, but she had confidence in her ability to wrap him round her little finger. As soon as her father was well away, she hastened out to the mews in search of her faithful John Coachman.

She cornered him in the harness room and shut the door against the prying eyes and ears of their one stableboy. Without preamble, she told the elderly man of her predicament. That is, of some of it. She prudently withheld Pontleby's outrageous offer of a *carte blanche*.

"Mr. Pontleby holds my father's vowels to an impossible amount," she said. "Because we have not the money to pay his debt, Sir Agramont is forcing me to marry a rich man whom I detest."

"Ah," said John. "So all us thought belowstairs."

Juliana frowned slightly. Domestics had ears the very walls would envy. She went on. "I have employed a—a—man to steal Papa's vowels back for me, but to no avail."

"Ah," said John again, relief cracking the rough granite of his complexion. "So that's the way of it. All them notes young Emily Jane took to that there low tavern."

"Yes, only his efforts have come to naught. I find I must get them back myself."

Suspicion, concern, and disapproval chased themselves over John's rocky features. He pursed his lips.

"No, miss."

"Yes, John. I must. You see, since he cannot pay, Papa demands that I marry the man or Mr. Pontleby will see us both in Fleet Street. Now," she continued, getting down to the real business at hand, "Mr. Pontleby is gone from Town for a few days. His house will be empty. I want you to drive me there at midnight tonight and stand guard outside his gate while I see if I cannot get inside. I know where he keeps those vowels."

"No, miss!"

"Yes, John," she repeated patiently. "If I can but remove them from his possession, I shall thereby save my father from ruination and myself from a life of misery bound to a horrid man."

The coachman argued in vain, for he was no match for his persuasive mistress. He finally agreed, much against his better judgement. Juliana, sternly repressing her own burgeoning misgivings, returned to her chamber and her favourite window-seat for a few serious thoughts.

THE WITCHING HOUR drew near, and Juliana donned her darkest gown and a pair of sturdy jean half-boots in case she had to climb the tree. Just as she prepared to leave, her door flew open and Emily Jane popped in like the cuckoo from a clock.

"'Ere now, Miss Julie!" she exclaimed. "What's all this John Coachman 'as been telling me? 'E's that upset!"

Juliana drew in a sharp breath and let it out slowly. She might have known. Devil take it, why could the man not keep his council? And to tell Emily Jane, of all people! She knew why, of course: his innate sense of what was right. His lady could not venture out at night unaccompanied by her abigail.

Emily Jane's next words confirmed it. "John Coachman says as 'ow it ain't the thing you should go out without me to give you countenance." She fell from her noble pedestal. "Asides, I wants to go, too! I wouldn't miss this fer the 'ole world!"

"This is not a picnic I'm attending," Juliana told her severely. "It will be very dangerous."

Emily Jane's eyes shone. "Oh, Miss Julie, I never robbed a 'ouse afore!"

"And you are not going to rob this one."

"Miss Julie!"

Emily Jane's lugubrious expression proved too much. Besides, Juliana admitted, the thought of someone else along was somehow comforting. Her coachman had to remain with the horses, but the abigail could wait outside whatever window she entered, to keep watch for a possible observer. Far better than enlisting the aid of, say, her parent. She pictured Sir Agramont in the role of her assistant and shuddered. By midnight, he would have been dipping rather deeply and be three parts disguised. Having John Coachman and Emily Jane on her team gave her a slight feeling of security. But very slight.

Taking Emily Jane into her confidence, she began to explain her plans.

JULIANA AND EMILY JANE stood in a deeply shadowed yew alley gazing at Pontleby's dark windows. Behind them, secreted by a tall hedgerow, John Coachman muttered and grumbled to his pair of uninterested horses.

The two girls walked as silently as they could towards the house. Emily Jane's dark uniform—she had left her apron in the carriage—and Juliana's own deep blue gown disappeared in the black of the night. Beside her, the pale oval of Emily Jane's face seemed to float among the trees until they stopped at the moonlit lawn. Unfortunately, it was very well-lit, for the moon was full.

"I'm that thirsty I'm like to die," the abigail whispered suddenly.

"How can you think of a thing like that at this moment?" Juliana wondered.

"I dunno, miss. Mayhaps it's all that salt."

"Salt? What salt?"

Emily Jane's feet scuffled in the leaves on the path. "I ate it," she mumbled.

Juliana threw up her hands. "What ever are you talking about?"

The abigail hastened to explain. "A 'ole thimbleful you 'as to eat without drinking no water afore going to bed so's you'll dream of your intended."

"Don't tell me you did that tonight!"

"'Ow was I to know we was going out? Lawks, Miss Julie, I be thirsty."

"You'll have to wait until we get home." Already running on sheer nerve, Juliana lost patience. She caught Emily Jane's hand and hurried her across the open space to the shelter of the ivy-covered brick walls of the house.

The only light within the building was a dim one in the back premises, no doubt in the servants' hall. The coast seemed clear. Now if only a window had been left unlatched somewhere...

They tiptoed around the house, Juliana trying the windows. As they came to the lower step of the terrace, with the huge tree described by her Corsair beside it, Emily Jane yelped. Juliana turned to shush her, and saw the abigail kiss first one thumb and then the other.

"What did you do?" she asked in a hoarse whisper. "Did you fall on your hands?"

"No, mum. I stubbed me toe."

"Then why—?"

"When you stubs your toe, if you kisses your thumb you sees your loved one afore dark."

"It's already dark. Besides, you are going to dream of him anyway."

Emily Jane limped after her. "I stubbed about three of 'em," she whispered. "I only 'ave two thumbs—do you think that's enough?"

"Do be quiet! We're passing the servants' wing and someone may still be about."

Juliana did not dare try for a window there, and she hurried on around the house. On the far side, another terrace stretched towards what might have been a rose garden. It was too dark to make out the identity of the shrubs, but chairs were placed as though inviting guests to admire the view. A row of French windows ran the entire length of the terrace, and adjuring Emily Jane to have the goodness not to crash into anything, Juliana crept over quietly and began checking the latches.

"Ah!" she breathed, as one gave before her touch. Thank goodness, one of Pontleby's domestics had been sadly remiss. She opened the floor-length window wide enough to slip inside. Emily Jane came right after her.

Juliana pushed her back out. "No, no! You are to wait here for me. If I am in trouble—if you hear me scream—you must be free to run to John Coachman for help."

"But, Miss Julie—"

"No! And keep your voice down. Do you wish us to be discovered? I need you out here. You are to be my look-out, a vitally important task. I dare not go in unless I know you are here to—to protect my escape route."

This satisfied Emily Jane. Almost. "Coo," she muttered. "I'd give me Sunday gown for a sip o' water."

"Shush! Just sit down and wait for me."

Dutifully, Emily Jane sat in one of the chairs near the windows.

Juliana moved inside, breathing a sigh of relief. All this evening needed for a thoroughly eventful finish would be for Emily Jane to knock over a table full of bric-à-brac before she could find those dratted vowels.

The room she entered was a parlour, liberally dotted with tables bearing crystal vases, silver picture frames, boxes wafting the odour of tobacco, and china ornaments which clinked together as she threaded her way. Once she crossed the floor, the light of the moon could penetrate no farther and she faced blackness. She continued on, feeling her way along a wall, around a settee, a carved chest—and the opening of a doorway.

She stepped through, greeted by that feeling one can receive in total darkness of being in a vast, empty space. A great hall. Now, if only she did not stumble against a suit of armour or the butler's dinner gong...

Her eyes became adjusted, and she grew aware of a faint glow high above her head. A wall sconce with a single taper at the head of a flight of stairs. She crept towards it, located the steps and began to climb. Halfway up, one of the treads gave out a dismal creak and she crouched against the bannister, horrified.

Nothing happened.

Calming her shattered nerves, Juliana began to climb again, reaching the landing on the first floor, where the wall sconce shed its dim glow. On her right, a corridor led past several closed doors. At the far end, a door stood ajar and she ran lightly towards it. Pushing it open, she peeked inside. The study! It must be, for there was a desk, gleaming softly in the moonlight from the window. Thankfully, she made for it—and behind her, a candle flickered alight.

She whirled about and Pontleby's voice purred from the shadows.

"Well, well," he said. "Not the visitor I expected, but a far more welcome one."

CHAPTER ELEVEN

JULIANA TURNED TO RUN, but Pontleby was between her and the door. He kicked it shut and leaned a shoulder against it negligently.

Shoving the image of a fainting Adorinda from her mind, she drew herself up. "Stand aside, sir. I wish to leave."

Pontleby smiled, and the candle on the table below his face lit his features in a satanic cast. "I'm afraid not," he said, shaking his head. "You've come of your own free will and you are going to stay overnight. Face it, my dear. You are ruined."

Juliana fought to control her swelling panic. "You would not dare keep me here!"

"Oh, but I would. Come, it won't be a bad life. I'll keep you in style. Clothes, jewels, your own carriage, and incidentally, I'll even cancel your father's debt to me. How can you refuse?"

Adorinda revived, her righteous principles of moral rectitude stiffening Juliana's spine. "Never!" declared the virtuous Gothic heroine.

Pontleby's eyebrows rose, increasing his devilish expression—and her terror. Did she face the Fate Worse Than Death?

"Then you lose on all counts," he said. "You will come to me willingly, or all the Polite World knows where you have spent this night and your father goes to prison as well. Think it over, Juliana."

Her voice quavered in spite of her efforts to put up a brave front. "You would not!"

"I might. We'll see. I believe I shall go out now and make the rounds of the clubs. I shall tell everyone I meet to expect a bit of interesting news on the morrow. Whether it will concern only you, or both you and your father, depends on your decision." He reached a hand behind him and opened the door. "By the by, the servants' hall is in the other wing. You may scream all you like, no one will hear. Until morning, Juliana."

He stepped back through the doorway, and she heard the key turn in the lock.

Oh, where was her masked Corsair when she needed him? Here she was, just like that idiotish Adorinda, locked in a tower—well, a study—by a dastardly villain. Now was when she should faint if she was ever to do so, but she had no time to waste on such Adorinda-like behaviour. She had to find a way to get free. In her panic, all thought of her father's vowels fled her mind. She had to escape!

If there had been a bed in the room, she could have knotted the sheets into a rope and escaped out the window—provided she could get it open. It was too high to climb through easily. She pulled over the desk chair, mounted it, and pushed on the unyielding casement. Probably, it had not been opened in years. She looked about for a tool with which to pry at the rusted latch. On Pontleby's desk was a complete set of writing accessories, including a large brass paper-knife. It proved just the thing.

A few minutes' work, several broken fingernails, and she crawled through, out onto a tiny balcony. The masked man's huge oak, lit by the full moon, spread its branches over her head. That meant she was on the wrong side of the great house to shout for Emily Jane.

She considered the tree. Gothic heroines were never so unladylike as to climb trees to escape their villains, but a mere ten years ago, Juliana's expertise in that direction had been the bane of her governess's existence. Surely the old skill remained and, thankfully, Pontleby hadn't expected a delicate female to attempt such a feat.

A low railing surrounded the balcony. Hitching up her skirts, she clambered up on it. The strongest branches of the tree were farther away than she'd thought, and the ground beneath even farther. She'd probably be killed, but it would be better than remaining here, a prisoner in the power of a fell villain. She hesitated, perched on the top rail like a roosting bird.

From the stable in the back of the house, she heard the clatter of hooves as Pontleby's curricle pulled out of the yard. The foul Count Valnescue was off to spread his vicious rumours. He must be foiled!

The one branch she thought heavy enough to bear her weight stretched towards the wall several feet below her. With both hands she grasped a lighter bough and leaned forward. She could almost touch the sturdier limb with the tip of one toe. She tightened her grip on the smaller branch. If she could swing a trifle to the left . . .

Commending her spirit to the Powers That Be, she pushed herself off the railing.

AN ENAMELLED SNUFF-BOX and an ebony-handled quizzing glass with a gold filigree frame were burning holes in the pockets of the Marquis of Ranceford. If Henry Pontleby truly had gone into the country, the pilfered items might not be missed until his return. If they were replaced they might not be missed at all. Much as he shrank from the task, Rance's conscience drove him to make the attempt. To his mind, the objects stolen by one who had illegally entered a home at his behest weighed far more heavily on his inherent sense of honour than did the recovery of a packet of vowels held for a dastardly purpose.

Even though the moon was full, he planned his second housebreaking for that very evening on the chance that Pontleby might not expect him so soon. Three a.m. was the hour selected. By that time, if a footman had been set to watch with a bird gun—he hoped it was of no larger a bore—the man might have fallen into a doze. Or even better, he might have given up and sneaked away to his own comfortable bed.

Too nervous to wait for so advanced an hour, he excused himself from a game of hazard at Brooks's shortly after midnight and strode off towards Covent Garden and the Nag's Head Inn, where he'd left his curricle and pair in Willy's care. He located the little hedge-bird easily, in Pacha's stall, and noted again the way the fractious beast had taken to his unlikely groom.

"I've wondered," Rance remarked, "what were you before you went on the high toby? I'll warrant it had to do with the prads."

"Yer right there, cocky." Willy removed the brim of his disreputable hat from Pacha's teeth and substituted a fistful of hay. "Stable-boy, I were, out Kensington way, till the ol' scum-scraper they 'ad as 'ead groom laid me orf."

"What had you filched from him?"

"Nuthin'!" Willy waxed indignant. "Nuth-blasted-in'! I found me a cigar wot was full 'alf left and the rum ol' cove twigged me ablowin' a cloud up in the 'ay-loft. Like to near turn me up by me toes, 'e did."

"Noth-blasted-ing to what I'll do if I catch you smoking near *my* hay," Rance informed him. "You might have burned down the entire mews."

"'At's wot 'e said when 'e thrun me down the ladder. I knows better now."

"I should hope so, if you're going to work round any of my horses."

Willy glanced up at him sideways, as though gauging his mood. "I reckon I'm ripe ter settle down." He gave Pacha an off-handed cuff on the nose to disengage the tail of his coat, and peered up at the marquis again.

"I needs to 'ave me some steady employment," he said, apparently to the horse, "iffen I gets legshackled."

"Miss Juliana Beveridge's abigail?" Rance considered Willy speculatively. Cleaned up, the man looked quite respectable, after his own fashion. And why not keep him in the family, so to speak? He seemed to be there already. "Have you indeed fixed your interest with the young, er, lady?"

"Naw. I ain't sure she'll 'ave me," said Willy, suddenly humble. "I 'opes mayhap she'll think seriouslike on it iffen I 'as a way o' earnin' 'er keep."

Rance grinned. "If we live through this evening, Willy, I'll see you in my stables." He slapped Pacha's black satin rump, forgetting. The horse threw its head and shied sideways, upsetting a water bucket into his manger. Willy dived to fish it out. Rance dived to retrieve his curly-brimmed beaver before it was trampled, and replaced it on his head. "Pacha, here," he continued calmly, "will need your tender ministrations. I cannot see him yielding to another groom."

Willy climbed out, adorned with scraps of hay and a glowing face. "Yer'll never regret it, me lord."

"I'll see to it that I don't," said Rance, assuming his most noble manner.

It had no effect on the beaming Willy. "Right yer are, me lord."

"Confound it, man, stop calling me that. Someone might hear. Do you know how to harness a pair?"

"Oh, yus, me, er, cocky. That were one o' me jobs."

The marquis let the "cocky" pass. It was safer. "Then hitch up the chestnuts while I change into my costume."

"Wuffor?" Willy sounded apprehensive. "We ain't bringin' that Quality biddy, be us?"

Rance thought quickly. "Dark clothes. I don't want to be seen. Or recognized," he added, remembering the mask. "Get on with it."

"Oh, aye."

"And be quiet. We don't want to rouse the whole place."

"They's already pretty roused," said Willy laconically, taking Ranceford's harness from the curricle. "Ain't never nuthin' else but, 'ere." He laid out the leathers in a manner professional enough to pass muster and went after the chestnut pair.

Rance dressed quickly in an empty stall and stowed his clothes under the curricle seat. In a short time, after he'd made a thorough check on Willy's work, he was turning his horses out the stableyard gate.

"Tool 'em round by front," ordered Willy, sitting up straight beside him. "So's all them poor sods wot 'as to stagger about on bandy pins'll cast their daylights on me ridin' in style."

They were passing the entrance to the Nag's Head before Rance could demur. He shrank behind Willy as a dozen or so raffish drunkards, lined up by the door, set up a cheer and tossed an assortment of ragged headgear into the air.

Willy negligently waved a regal hand with a dignity surpassing Prinny himself. He settled back with a satisfied sigh. "Ah-h."

"Enjoyed that, did you?" the marquis asked, grim.

Willy beamed. "That I done. Gives me a proper send-off, it does. Now they knows wot I tole 'em is proper sooth."

"I suppose you told *everyone* we were going out tonight."

Rance's words had an ominous ring which was lost on Willy, who widened innocent eyes. "O' course I did. Otherway, they wun't 'ave knowed and mebbe never 'ave seed me settin' up 'ere in a flash carriage."

"And did you tell them *where* we were going and *why?*"

"They wun't 'ave paid no never-mind."

Muttering to himself, Rance drove on. His uneasiness grew as they approached Pontleby's home. "They are not the only ones who know," he remarked. "I believe we are expected. That is, I am. The owner of the house is out of Town, but I suspect he may have set a guard."

"The cove o' the crib fly, eh? We'd best comport us cautiouslike," Willy said mildly. He fished in a pocket and removed a filthy cloth sack containing a small lumpy object. "Ball o' lead," he explained. "Saves a deal o' trouble."

Rance gritted his teeth, remembering Pontleby lying in the gutter. "Put that back."

"Iffen yer say so." Willy shrugged. "Never 'urts to be on the ready."

Oh, hell. Only the fact that he was committed and on his way kept Ranceford going. That, and his pride—and the thought of Juliana in his arms should he succeed. One-eye Willyum might prove a liability, but without him, this venture was probably doomed to failure. Milling kens, to quote Willy, was definitely not his lay.

He had planned to leave his curricle partly hidden by the tall hedge where he had left it after the dinner with Pontleby, but another carriage waited there already. Its coachman paced nervously in the moonlight. Ranceford pulled up behind and swung to the ground, forgetting he wore his Corsair rig, mask and all. Oh, the devil, the man would take him for a brigand!

Instead, the distraught coachman ran to him, catching his hand. "Oh, sir, thanks be you'm come! Yer'll get 'er out!"

Rance cursed aloud, gripped by a horrid foreboding. He had no need to ask the identity of "'er." "What the devil is she up to now?" he demanded.

"Never shoulda let 'er talk me inter it," the man moaned, shaking his head. "She's gorn in there atter them vowels o' 'er papa's."

Damnation! "How could you have permitted it? You must have known something would happen!"

Had he a joint stool, Rance could have combed the old coachman's hair with it.

"She'm a very determined lady, sir. Allus 'as been. But Emily Jane is wi'er.''

"A hell of a help that will be. How long has Miss Beveridge been in there?''

"Seems hours, sir.''

Allowing for the man's nerves, it could be any time from ten minutes to twenty. "Come on, Willy, we're going after her. Where are you? Oh.'' He spotted Willyum, a shadow drifting ahead of him down the drive, and ran to catch up.

Silently, they crept around the darkened house to the terrace where Pontleby had pointed out the huge oak tree, the landmark Rance had mentioned to Juliana. Candlelight glimmered faintly in the upstairs study window. Could the blasted girl be up there?

Rance grabbed Willy's arm and pulled him to a halt under the tree. Someone, or something, struggled about in the boughs above them. As they stared, a branch broke with a crack like a pistol shot. A body plummeted down through the leaves.

Rance leapt forward and caught a tangled mass of skirts and flailing arms and legs. The momentum knocked the wind from him, sprawling him on the ground. The mass landed on his chest and resolved into a female, her lungs expanding for a frantic scream.

He clamped a hand over her mouth, gasping for breath. "Hush, damn it! It's me!''

Juliana flung her arms about his neck, with a tiny sound suspiciously like a choking sob. He managed to sit up, cuddling her shaking form while she buried her face in his shoulder.

Her voice came to him, muffled by his cape. "I *knew* you'd come." She lifted her head. "But you are a trifle late. I've rescued myself."

"Rescued! If I hadn't been under you, you'd have broken your fool neck! What the devil do you think you're up to? Why couldn't you wait for me?"

"How was I to know you'd really come?"

"I am the hero in this melodrama, am I not? So let me handle my part and you take care of yours."

She grinned at him, tightening the arms about his neck. "Faint, then, shall I?"

"Now why would you do a silly thing like that?"

One-eye Willyum was standing over them, peering down at what he could see of Juliana in the moonlight. "So this 'ere's yer gentry mort," he observed. "Bang up. Yer 'as good taste."

Juliana hastily scrambled to her feet, pulling down her skirts. She leaned towards the former highwayman, examining his face. "You must be One-eye Willyum. And you do have two eyes, just as Emily Jane said. Emily Jane!" She turned to Rance, who had risen and was shaking the dust from his cape. "She's waiting for me around on the other side. I must go to her at once."

Willy was already off. "I'll fetch her, miss." He vanished silently around the house.

Rance, now that he knew Juliana was unhurt, naturally was furious. "What the devil are you doing here, anyway? Whatever made you try to climb that tree?"

"I was climbing down, not up. I was escaping. I thought I'd best get those vowels myself, for I was afraid you would come here and get caught, and I could not let you be hanged for a common thief because of me."

Ranceford snorted. "So you planned to be hanged in my stead? Of all the addlepated notions!"

His anger ignited hers. "I assure you, Henry Pontleby has no intention of hanging me! Far from it. He was up there in his study waiting, and he locked me in and said I had to stay all night so I would be ruined unless I came to him willingly."

He stiffened beside her, frozen with quite another rage. "The man must be desperate indeed to go to such lengths to force you to marry him."

"He—he said marriage was not his intention."

"I see." Ranceford spoke very quietly. "I suspected as much." His eyes, in the holes of his black mask, blazed with a cold fire in the moonlight. White lines formed about his mouth. "My seconds will call on him in the morning."

"No!" She clutched at his shirt front. "*No!* None of this must ever be known! Do you wish to make me the subject of every gossip-monger's on-dit?"

She had a valid point, albeit one he could not like. Once more he must hold back, though he felt close to murder. Henry Pontleby would rue this day.

WITH THE CONSTERNATION of one who has opened a door and inadvertently loosed a tiger, Juliana stared at him, appalled at the transformation of the gentle man she knew. His cold fury vibrated in the air about them, and she knew a fear deeper than any she'd ever known before: fear for the man who had turned to a statue carved in ice.

Dear heaven, what had she done? She should never have told him of Pontleby's foul intentions. Her terror for her masked Corsair was real. He'd find another excuse to challenge the man. Would he kill Pontleby? And be exiled, or tried for murder? In mounting horror, she threw her arms about him. She could not lose him now, not when she'd just realized how all-important a part of her life he'd become.

As though aware of her once more, he relaxed. His tense arms softened, encircling her in a welcome warmth. His voice, carefully controlled, sounded comfortingly normal. "I believe I must arrange a suitable downfall for your Count Valnescue."

Juliana choked on a tiny giggle of relief. "Oh, please do. But pray do not kill him."

He managed a smile. "Killing would be too good for such a villain. Never fear, I shall devise something suitable." He tipped up her chin and kissed the end of her nose, which seemed to give him an excellent idea. Folding her closer, he sought and found her lips.

After some little time, he raised his head, drawing a deep, satisfied breath. "My dearest girl, this is all well and good—absolutely delightful, in fact—but I take it you still do not have your father's vowels. Should we not go after them?"

"The vowels! Oh, no! How could I have been so hen-witted! I was there, locked in that study, and my only thought was to escape. I fear I panicked like a hare-brained Adorinda and all sense fled from my mind!"

"Just like a female." He seemed obscurely pleased and patted her on the head. "Never mind. I must go back in there in any case to replace a few objects Willy removed on our last visit. Tell me, where is Pontleby now? I collect he is not in his study, since you managed to escape."

It was time to return to reality. Juliana gave up her attempts to restore order to her chaotic curls and even more chaotic feelings. "He has gone to his clubs. I heard his curricle drive off while I was up in that tree." She refrained from telling him *why* Pontleby went and what news he planned to spread. She'd not stir up *that* hornet's nest again. "He seemed to think I would wait patiently up there until his return," she finished.

"I daresay he will be sorry to find you gone. In fact," he added, grim, "I shall see to it. While no one is now on guard, I'd best be on my way." He peered into the shadows at the end of the terrace. "Where is that da-dratted—Willyum? He is gone a long while."

As he spoke, Willy materialized around the corner of the house. He held his hat in one hand and led Emily Jane by the other. Both seemed unaccustomedly self-conscious.

"What the h—what have you been doing?" Rance demanded. "You've been a devil of a time."

Emily Jane succumbed to a fit of the giggles, and would have thrown her apron over her head, had she not left it behind.

Willy hastily dropped her hand. "This 'ere ain't the place fer argle-bargle," he blustered. "Be we goin' in or ain't we?"

"We are," Rance assured him, looking up at the study window with some doubt. "However, I'm not going to climb that tree."

Willy sniffed. "I told yer of a easy way. Foller me." He headed off around the corner, the others behind him.

As they neared the kitchen quarters, he stopped so suddenly that Rance stepped on his heels. Juliana bumped into Rance and his arm went about her. From that safe port, she peeked over Willy's shoulder and saw what had arrested the little thief. Something was happening at one of the windows.

Huddling in a tight group against the wall of the house, they watched as one of Pontleby's maids clambered out, found footing on a stack of boxes and an old bench, and scuttled across the back garden to a potting shed.

"'At's 'er," whispered Willy. "Gorn to meet 'er under-gardener. We'ums got a good 'our."

"How do you know?" Rance demanded, *sotto voce*.

"'At's 'ow long it took us'n."

Juliana felt Rance's quick glance at her and returned it with one innocently unaware. Emily Jane, far less unaware, took it in stride.

The scullery maid vanished into the shed. "Come along, then," said Willy and started towards the window.

"We are to climb through that?" Rance asked. "All right." He turned to Juliana. "You and your maid wait here. We should not be long."

"We certainly will not wait! I must come! I know the way." There ensued a short, sharp, whispered altercation, and in the end all four crept up to the bench with the stacked boxes. The masked man and Willy went in first. When it was her turn, Emily Jane started to speak.

Juliana shushed her. "We shall let the men handle this."

"But—"

"Gentlemen, or at least males, always know best."

"Yes'm, but—"

"Up you go."

Emily Jane upped, still making doubtful protests as she climbed onto the bench.

From within, Juliana heard a muttered curse, and hesitated outside the window, but it seemed merely that a dry sink stood immediately below inside and, partly blinded by his mask, her Corsair had stepped into a tub of cold water. She pushed Emily Jane through, gathered up her skirts and crawled in after her.

Little of the bright moonlight penetrated within. She stood still, waiting for her eyes to become attuned to the darkness. The masked man had brought a candle and his Patent Ethereal Matches. When the candle flared alight, she squeaked, her nerves still jumpy from the encounter with Pontleby. She was warned to silence, and he led them through what appeared to be a pantry. After waiting for Emily Jane, who stopped for a dipper of water, they proceeded down a corridor, pushed past a pair of swinging baize doors and entered the great hall Juliana had been in before.

Sounds of movement came from a room on their left.

"Dowse the glim!" Willy whispered, as another candle shone in the doorway.

They were near the staircase and crouched beside it in the shadows. The candle wavered across the hall, held in the hands of an unsteady butler making his rounds.

"'Im's tap-hackled!" Willy hissed, indignant. "'E's been at them fancy bottles they leave about in the eatin' room!"

"I still be that thirsty you wunt believe," Emily Jane complained to him.

Juliana poked her in the ribs. "Do be quiet! Both of you!"

The butler, his rounds completed, re-entered the hall and they pressed closer to the staircase, though from the aroma of alcohol wafting towards them as the man passed by within a few yards, they need not have worried.

Juliana felt her Corsair leave her side as soon as the butler blundered through the baize doors. He dropped a couple of metal objects onto a chest. "Willy's loot," he explained, nearly inaudibly. "That's done. Now for the study."

Clinging together like mountain climbers, they crept up the stairs.

"There is a tread which creaks," Juliana remembered. "Look out for it."

"Where?" the masked man asked as he stepped on it. "Damnation!"

Juliana nodded in the dark. "Yes, there. That one."

He said something else, under his breath, and Willy whistled softly.

"You'm got a way wi' words, cocky."

"I'm sorry," whispered Juliana. "Unfortunately, I neglected to count so I'd know which one it was. I hadn't thought to come this way again."

He squeezed her hand. "I hear no sounds of pursuit. You're forgiven." They reached the first landing. "Now which way?"

Juliana led them down the corridor to the study door. It was still locked and, to her dismay, she saw that Pontleby had taken away the key. Her Corsair had something else to say, but so quietly she heard only his expelled breath.

One-eye Willyum proved his worth. "Make me a light, cocky, and 'old it close." He pulled a handful of tiny metal picks from his pocket and worked on the lock by the light of their candle. In a surprisingly few minutes, he pushed the door open.

"Coo!" Emily Jane murmured admiringly. "Ain't you the smart one."

"Aw," Willy muttered, standing aside to let them enter.

Juliana was already at the desk, pawing through the pigeon-holes. "They are not here!" she wailed.

She was set gently aside. "Let me try. Usually there is a secret drawer. Ah, here it is." There was a soft click and the candlelight shone on a tiny panel sliding outward. In a cache inside were a number of sheets of paper. He handed them to her. "Are these the ones?"

Juliana leafed through them with trembling fingers, recognizing her father's hand. Mentally, she tallied the total and shuddered. Sir Agramont had not exaggerated. She folded the sheets quickly and tucked them into her bodice, turning away. As she did so, the masked man took something from his pocket and placed it in the open secret drawer.

"All right, let us depart—silently!" The black-caped figure tucked an arm about her and became a shadow in the sudden darkness when he blew out the candle.

One-eye Willyum hesitated by the desk, his hand hovering over the open drawer which now contained a thick roll of soft. His fingers flickered, and a new bulge appeared in his pocket. He hurried after them.

They made their way back down to the kitchen premises, and stopped. A dim glow came from the area leading to the pantry where they had come in. Inside, a candle on the table reflected the thundercloud countenance of Willy's scullery maid. A decanter of brandy from the dining-room was in one of her hands, a half-empty glass in the other.

"'Ad a fight wi'er boy-friend," Willy opined in a stage whisper as they shrank back out into the corridor. "She'm like to sit there fer 'ours. Us'll 'ave ter find 'nother way out."

"There's a French door open in the side parlour," Juliana offered. "I came in that way."

Her hero turned on her. "Why the devil did you not tell me before we climbed through that da—confounded window?"

Juliana gazed up at him soulfully, fluttering her eyelashes and assuming the innocent mien of the hapless Adorinda.

"Why, I did not wish to spoil your fun, and besides, you told me to keep my—"

"Enough," he interrupted with a rueful grin. "I daresay I deserved it."

They had reached the great hall once more and Emily Jane, who had been silent for too long, complained again. "I wish we coulda got into that kitchen again. I'm that thirsty—"

Willy rose to the occasion. "Eatin' room's over this way. Iffen that boozin' butler 'as left any, some o' them fancy bottles is doubtless 'arf full."

Before they could stop him, he barged off across the hall—straight into the dinner gong. His ears ringing, he staggered back, bumping into Emily Jane, who crashed into a suit of armour at the foot of the stairs.

The resultant din could have awakened the dead.

CHAPTER TWELVE

JULIANA DIVED into the scattered armour and extricated Emily Jane. Pulling her dazed abigail along, she dashed across the hall towards an open door from which moonlight shone through undrawn curtains.

"In here!" she shrieked. "This is where I came in!"

Rance tore after her, herding the stunned Willy in front of him. All four met in a crush at the door and burst into the room like corks from a shaken champagne bottle. Upsetting two small tables and a spindly chair on her way, Juliana ran for the central French window.

The tipsy butler, ever mindful of his duties, had already made for it.

"Oh, no! He bolted it!" she cried.

Rance had out his Ethereal Matches and struck his candle alight. "Hold this for me," he ordered, handing the candle to Juliana. "I'll get the bolt open."

Shouts and running feet sounded from the servants' wing.

"Oh, hurry!" Juliana squeaked, nervously waving the flaming candle. She waved it too close to the curtains and in seconds a panel was ablaze.

It was no time for finesse. Ranceford put a booted foot through the glass panes, splintering the wooden frames. Peeling off his Corsair cloak, he threw it over the broken glass, grabbed Juliana and shoved her outside.

Her head came back in. "But the fire—"

"Don't give it a thought. We've already sounded an alarm. Run!" he yelled. Two footmen were already upon them. Willy and Emily Jane went out the window after Juliana, leaving the masked Corsair at bay.

Rance started to draw his costume sword. Good Lord, what was he thinking to be drawing steel? These men were unarmed! He dropped the sword back into its scabbard, barely in time to land his first opponent a wisty castor which knocked him into a china cabinet. The second he downed with a leveller to the jaw. He leapt through the shattered window, caught up his precious cape, and pounded down the gravel drive. Shouts of *"Fire!"* followed him.

Ahead, he saw John Coachman catch up Juliana and throw her into the carriage, Emily Jane scrambling after her. One-eye Willyum had taken it on his toes around the hedgerow and vanished. Hastily untying his pair, Rance bounded into his curricle, gave the horses the office, and drove *ventre à terre* for home.

A great weight lifted from his shoulders. Juliana had her blasted vowels at last—that is, if the confounded girl hadn't lost them as they fled....

JULIANA HAD THE VOWELS. And she awoke next morning with something else, something she hugged in her heart—the knowledge that she was in love.

She had long suspected that she was developing a *tendre* for her dashing Corsair, but thought it a silly infatuation only, a passing fancy she would outgrow, for her father had impressed on her from childhood that it was her duty to wed a fortune. But now—now she was free, to marry where she would. She had those dreadful vowels, and surely Sir Agramont would not dare browbeat her again after the trouble he had caused with his foolhardy gaming.

But she was less foolish? She didn't care. Like the simpering Adorinda, she had fallen under the spell of a swashbuckling romantic. Her masked hero had rescued her from the Fate Worse Than Death just as in a Gothic novel. He had slain—figuratively, she prayed—her dragon, like a true knight in shining armour.

Thinking of armour, she giggled, remembering One-eye Willyum and Emily Jane rolling about the floor amid the scattered gorgets, gauntlets, and greaves. What a night it had been! One she could not confide to a soul, but her memories filled her inside with sweetness and light like the cream in a luscious puff pastry.

Sir Agramont did not yet know they were saved, for he was snoring in his bed when she and Emily Jane finally reached home. Juliana could hardly contain herself until he awakened and she could proudly present him with those fateful papers. Rummaging in one of her dressing-table drawers, she found a length of pink satin ribbon and tied it round the folded sheets in a lovely bow.

Her chamber door opened suddenly and Emily Jane stood on the threshold, her apron rolled about her clasped hands and her face flushed with an overwhelming pride and joy.

"Miss Julie, 'e done it!"

Juliana set down the packet of vowels. "Who? And did what?"

"Mr. Willyum. 'E's belowstairs."

It took only a moment for Juliana to decipher this new title. "One-eye Willyum?" The masked man's courier! Emily Jane's pleasure thrilled through her. "Is he coming? Has he sent me a message?"

"No'm. Miss Julie, Willyum come to offer for me!"

"Emily Jane!" Juliana exclaimed, let down and shocked. "You cannot marry a common thief!"

The abigail stuck out a stubborn lip. "'Ow can we fault 'im when only last night we done a bit o' 'ousebreaking ourselves?" She came into the room, her hands still beneath her apron. "Miss Julie, 'e's left all that. All what 'e needs is a good woman to turn 'im about."

Truly, love was blind. Juliana remembered something else. "That scullery maid—"

Emily Jane sniffed. "No better than she should be, that one. Seducted 'im, is what she did. Asides, 'e ain't no country bumpkin, Miss Julie. 'E's a Man o' the Town, 'e is," she announced proudly.

Juliana gave up on that score. "But he is still a thief."

"'E won't do none o' that no more when I gets 'old o' 'im. 'E'll know better," she added darkly. "And that's what I come up 'ere for." Her hands came out of the apron and she held out a roll of paper money. "'E said to give this 'ere to you."

Uncomprehending, Juliana looked at the money. Had Willy robbed the Bank of England? "Where did that come from?"

"When your man took them vowels, 'e put this in that bitty drawer, as payment like, and Willy says as 'ow 'e couldn't resist the sight o' all that rhino. Only 'is conscience won't let 'im keep it. 'E wants you should give it back 'cause 'e's feared your masked man will wash 'is 'ands o' 'im, lessen you speaks a good word and explains. 'E swears 'e'll never do no prig-gin' agin." Emily Jane's lips set in a grim line. "I'm not weddin' no thief, and 'e knows it."

Juliana accepted the thick roll. All that money! It must be every penny he had. She drew a deep breath. The honour of the man! He would not stoop to steal-ing those dratted vowels—but she had to give his money back to him. She could not allow him to beg-gar himself for her regrettable father. But could she convince him to take it? Or—oh, no!—would he in-sist on going once more to Pontleby's study to replace it in that secret drawer? He wouldn't! Or would he?

Emily Jane was backing towards the door. "Would you be wanting me for summat?"

Juliana shook her head absently, her mind on the nobility of her hero.

"Then iffen it's all right wi' you," said the abigail, trotting out the door, "I'll be gettin' on down to my Willyum and tell 'im you gives your approval."

So, Emily Jane had found her Prince Charming in the unlikely figure of a former—she hoped—highwayman. What about her own Prince? She shoved the money under her pillow and drifted back to her window-seat. Would he come to her in the garden tonight? She felt an uneasy qualm. They had the vowels. Their quest was completed. Suppose he did not come?

And if he did come—would he offer for her again after the way she had laughed at him before? She sat up straight. Why, in that case, she'd take a page from the book of Willyum's scullery maid, rather than one from *Adorinda,* and "seduct" him.

Picking up the packet of vowels with its gay ribbon bow, she went in search of her father. She located him in his bedchamber, downing a cup of hot chocolate. She presented him with vowels...and came up against a stone wall.

"I cannot take those! You must return them at once!" Sir Agramont declared, appalled. "A gaming debt is one of honour! All the ton knows I owe Pontleby! Give them back to him at once and I shall pay him as soon as you wed Ranceford—if you will not go to Pontleby." A look of horrified suspicion crossed his face. "Juliana! How did you get these?"

She was as shocked as he by the suggestion. "Nonsense, Papa! No such thing. A—a friend retrieved them for me."

"Then he must retrieve them back! I am honourbound to pay my debts. All the Polite World expects it of me."

Men and their idiotic honour! "And you mean to pay them with *me?* You will not! There must be another way. Papa, have you never thought a man of Pontleby's ilk may have cheated you with loaded dice? Did you not tell me he had the devil's own luck?"

"I admit the thought crossed my mind at the time, but I dismissed it immediately. A man of his ilk, indeed!" he blustered. "Henry Pontleby is a gentlemen. How can you speak so of a man of undoubted honour? Did he not offer to marry you in place of payment?"

Juliana bit her tongue to keep from making the answer which hovered on its slippery tip. Turning on her heel, she quit his presence.

Now what was she to do?

RANCE NO LONGER waited to be sent for; he took it for granted his Adorinda would be in the garden at midnight. All should now be well with Sir Agramont, and he meant to stake his all, proposing she marry her Corsair instead of the wealthy Marquis of Ranceford. He wanted her more than life itself, but only if she truly wanted him, not his title and fortune, for that would bring a pain he could not bear. He worried as he rode Pacha out of the stableyard of the Nag's Head. Now that she had those vowels, she would have no need to wed. Suppose she turned him down—or refused both of them?

Of his own feelings, he had no doubt whatsoever. No female could ever take the place of his Adorinda. Lady Catherine? She would have fainted dead away had a man made her so shocking a proposition. And at the thought of Lady Catherine climbing down that tree, he laughed aloud, startling Pacha into nearly unseating him. No, it was Adorinda or no one. She *had* to say yes to the Corsair.

Juliana was waiting, pacing back and forth in front of the garden bench when he arrived. Before he even secured Pacha to Prometheus's left leg, she began to pour out the story of her father's idiotic sense of honour.

Rance swept her into his arms. First things first. "Now," he said when he raised his head at last, "what's all this?"

She was near tears, but of anger and exasperation. "Papa won't take them," she cried, handing him the pink-ribboned packet of vowels. "He says gaming debts are a matter of honour. He says we must give them back."

Rance shook his head. "No, no. It's all right. I paid for them. The full amount."

"It's not all right." She caught up the roll of flimsies she'd left on the bench. "Here is your money.

Perhaps even all of it. Emily Jane took it from Willyum, who took it from that drawer.''

He stared at the money. ''Oh, hell and the devil confound it. Now I must return it to Pontleby. Blast Willyum!''

''You can't go back to his house! Not after what happened last night!''

''No, indeed. Not even for the pleasure of climbing his tree. I'll have to find some other way.''

''Why? Why must you take such a risk? Papa even admits he suspected Pontleby's dice may have been queered! The man doesn't deserve to be paid!''

He took her shoulders and shook her gently. ''He must be repaid, Adorinda, my love. I will not be a party to outright thievery. It is a matter of honour.''

''Honour! Men!'' Juliana stamped her foot in frustration. ''Take the vowels, then. Take your money. Do whatever you please!''

''Certainly.'' He drew her into his arms and kissed her long and thoroughly. ''This pleases me very much,'' he whispered into her ear. ''I plan to continue it, but at a later date. I'll be back tomorrow night and this time I shall have all settled. Hold on to those vowels.''

He released her, placed a final soft kiss on the tip of her nose, and mounted Pacha. The night was still young by Town standards, and he might yet find Pontleby in one of the clubs. He stood in the man's debt, and he must clear his account before he could mill the villain down and stamp on the remains.

Pausing at the Nag's Head only long enough to stable Pacha and change into his regular evening garb, he proceeded on a tour of the clubs and gaming hells. He finally ran Pontleby to earth in a particularly unsavoury house, in the vicinity of Pall Mall, where private wagers were permitted.

Standing in the doorway, he watched the man casting dice, and struggled to control an urge to stride up, seize Pontleby by the throat and strangle him on the spot. Only the knowledge that Juliana's reputation was at stake held him back from this delightful exercise. He could not be the cause of linking her name with a public brawl.

The thick roll of soft weighed heavily in his pocket and a plan formed in his mind. Why not challenge Pontleby to a game? He could lose the amount of the vowels to him, thus both clearing his conscience and creating an excuse to provoke a quarrel. His fists clenched into serviceable bunches of fives in anticipation.

Pontleby was dicing in a furious temper, the luck going badly against him. Had Rance not been regarding him so closely, he might have missed what happened next. As it was, the marquis drew in a hissing breath as he caught the surreptitious bit of sleight of hand by which Pontleby introduced a new pair of dice into the game. Pontleby's luck bettered at once, so after enough throws to establish an indisputable lead, Pontleby just as easily switched the dice back again.

So, Sir Agramont was right and the man was a cheat! This changed matters considerably. If it could be proven, those vowels of old Beveridge's—and no doubt those of countless others—would not be worth the paper on which they were written.

Rance stepped up to the table and swept Pontleby's winnings to one side. "Wait," he told the man's startled opponent. "I'll be but a few minutes."

Pontleby raised his head slowly and stared at Rance, his eyes ugly. "My Lord Ranceford," he said. "You'll pay for that china cabinet. Also my door and my curtains."

The Marquis of Ranceford's eyebrows rose. "I cannot imagine to what you refer."

"Can you not?" Pontleby's voice was a snarl. "You once offered to play me for some papers I held. I'll play you now, for the same stakes."

Rance's smile felt thin as a knife slash on his wooden face. "Then let it be dice." He picked up a die and tossed it from hand to hand. "I understand that is your game of preference." He saw the flash of triumph in the other's eyes, though it was quickly hidden. He cast the die he held and waited for Pontleby to throw for first.

The man took no chances. He picked up the dice from the table, rattled them in his hand, and reached into his coat pocket for his snuff-box, the act Rance had seen before.

Rance's hand shot out, gripping Pontleby's wrist until the painful pressure caused him to drop the snuff-box—and a pair of dice. He caught them up before Pontleby could seize them, and shouted for the proprietor to bring him a hammer.

"You dare!" White-faced, Pontleby bared his teeth. "I'll swallow no such insult! I demand satisfaction, Ranceford."

"Certainly," said Rance. "With the greatest of pleasure. I'll be with you as soon as I smash these dice."

Pontleby tore loose the wrist Rance still gripped and fled from the room, a ruined man. The hammer arrived, and Rance broke open the dice, displaying the lead weights within to the players who had crowded round the table.

SIR AGRAMONT brought the news to Juliana the next evening.

Word of Pontleby's flight to the Continent had spread on a flood tide through London's clubs and swept her father back to Beveridge House at an uncommon early hour. He burst into the parlour where Juliana was once again reading over the touching love scene at the end of volume 3.

She sprang to her feet in dismay, *Adorinda* falling to the floor unnoticed.

"What are you doing home so early?" she demanded, horrified. How could she slip out of the house at midnight if he were at home?

"It is Pontleby!" he crowed. "Ruined! Caught cheating in one of the clubs! And can you doubt it? Did I not tell you his dice were uphills?"

Juliana's thoughts immediately flew to her masked man. How had he managed this? If he had... "Are you sure, Papa?"

"It must be true." He picked up her book and leafed through some pages without looking at them. "Already a notice has been pinned on the board at Craghill's—you know the sort of thing, for I have been expecting one myself—an Auction to be Held of the Property of a Gentleman of Fashion Lately Gone to the Continent. It can only be Pontleby! They say the proceeds are to benefit those whom he cheated."

He dropped *Adorinda* back on the floor and circled the room, his mind at work. "He has some unexceptionable wines in his cellar.... I wonder if it is known that I have not yet paid my debt to him. I have back my vowels—you did retain them, did you not, my dear? I can present them as evidence and who can tell if perhaps... well, well, be that as it may. I could make ready use of such a windfall."

Juliana had been trying to speak, and she now broke in. "Who is responsible for exposing him? Do you know the man?"

"Now there is a coincidence! I have not told you all. It is Ranceford who has pulled our chestnuts from the fire."

"Ranceford!" Juliana's heart sank. Not her Corsair!

"I must have told him I suspected Pontleby's dice were queered," Sir Agramont went on, for he believed in giving credit where it was due. "I met him tonight and you must know I thanked him right heartily. I near swooned with relief on hearing the news."

"Oh, Papa, as do I!" For Juliana was sure her father had learned a valuable lesson. "And I pray you will finally give up gaming."

"What? What? Nonsense, my dear. A streak of bad luck, that is all. I have come about as I assured you I would. But, see here, my girl. You have weathered this incident without harm, but I mean to see you are never in such a situation again. I don't know how you obtained my vowels and I daresay I'd rather not know, but I have decided you must be safely married and at once. It is fortunate indeed that I have already accepted the offer of Lord Ranceford."

"Father! You cannot! You would not!"

"I can. I would. I have. Trust me, my daughter, I have your best interests at heart. He is the ideal man for us—you. A grand title, impeccable lineage, and great wealth."

"I care nothing for those attributes! Papa, I cannot love that man."

"What's love to do with it? Hear me, Juliana. He has solved our problem and saved our ancestral home—for the time being. But we have not the finances to keep it up. You must marry a fortune or we shall end up in Fleet Street yet."

"Papa, I cannot marry a stranger."

"As for that, he won't be a stranger long. You are to be wed in our family chapel in three weeks' time. I fixed all with Ranceford this evening. I shall call on Amelia Robertshaw to make the arrangements. It will be no bother to her, she dotes on such flummery celebrations." He drifted out the door, his mind taken up with another possibility. "I wonder what sort of settlement he plans to make...."

That is something you will never know, Juliana told his vanishing coattails, but silently. It was still two hours to midnight. She picked up *Adorinda,* upside down, and stared blindly at a page. She would *not* marry a cold, haughty, dull marquis. Not if her masked hero would aid her escape.

THE CORSAIR went to his meeting at midnight prepared to go down on one knee and formally beg Miss Beveridge for the honour of her hand in marriage. The matter was taken out of his hands.

She ran to meet him, throwing herself onto his chest, her arms about his neck. There was only one thing to do, so he did it.

When he returned to earth, he smoothed the hair back from her forehead with a gentle hand. "Now what calamity has occurred?" he asked.

"Papa says I am to wed Ranceford after all! We are obligated, for he is the one who finally saved us. And Papa will not cease his gaming, so he says I must marry his lordship, for without a fortune Papa will not survive another such crisis.''

Ranceford thought Sir Agramont's survival to be of not much account, but possibly it was important to his daughter. Not so, he found a moment later.

"I am going to run away!" she announced.

"Run away?"

"Yes. With you."

Rance steadied himself against the statue of Prometheus to which he had just hitched Pacha. The Corsair had won. His triumphant heart pounded so he could hardly speak. He took a deep breath, forcing his voice to steady.

"I see. In that case, my Adorinda, we must conceive a proper plot for our melodrama. I shall carry you off at the altar, of course—it is the only thing for us to do. Let me see. I have a deal of arrangements to make. In the meantime, I suggest you accept the lordship's offer."

"What?"

"You must seem willing, right up to the ceremony, for we do not wish to arouse your father's suspicions. If you go along with his plans, it will keep him quiet until we strike."

She still hesitated. "But Ranceford—I feel sorry for him. Will he not be furious?"

"No, no, believe me, the man will be quite relieved to be jilted."

She nodded wisely. "Because of Papa. Do you think Ranceford already has regrets?"

"I admit your father is a concern, but it is time and more that you have your own life. Your father will survive. He has a small competence, and without you to support, he can pay off some of his debts and be comfortable in his old age."

"Money! It is the cause of all my evils."

"Speaking of which..." He dug into a pocket and removed a roll of bills. "I did not feel a need to return this to Pontleby. I shall give it to Willy for a wedding present."

"All of that! Let me give it to Emily Jane. I imagine she'll put it to far better use than would your One-eye Willyum."

"Aye, maybe she will buy the Nag's Head for him, and I shall have a permanent home for my horse. So, all is settled."

Juliana still seemed worried. "The wedding is to take place in three weeks' time. You won't fail me?"

"I'll be there, I swear it. And I promise you shall not marry against your will."

"And you'll carry me off across your saddle-bow like Lochinvar?" She clasped her hands. "Oh, do! But what shall I do after?"

"Why, marry me. Not if you don't wish to, of course."

"Oh, yes, it is of all things the one wish of my life!"

She was in his arms again; he had no knowledge of how it happened, but he did not waste the opportunity. After a time, she buried her face in his shoulder with an Adorinda-like die-away sigh.

"My hero! I would rather live out our Gothic novel in a hovel with you than be a princess in a castle."

"Or a marchioness in a London town-house? Juliana, are you sure?"

"I want only my Corsair. Never change, my love."

He hugged her close. "By God, no. I shall always be the man I am now."

"Then I ask no more. To—to the devil with that odious, stiff-rumped Lord Ranceford."

Odious, was he? And stiff-rumped! "Is that not a bit harsh? After all, he is merely a bit player in our drama."

She snuggled against him with a tiny purr of contentment. "I suppose he may live, but not with me."

He gave the top of her head an enigmatic glance. "We'll see. You are quite sure I'll make a satisfactory substitute?"

Raising her face, she smiled at him fondly. "I'll accept no substitute for you."

He kissed the tip of her nose. "In that case, I'll see you at your wedding."

And you, my Adorinda, he promised himself, *shall finally see me!*

CHAPTER THIRTEEN

THE WEDDING PLANS went forward at Beveridge House under the firm guidance of Lady Amelia Robertshaw. Sir Agramont, needless to say, was in high gig.

"A tidy settlement!" he crowed. "Ranceford has invested it in the Funds. The interest, added to my small competency, will provide me with a comfortable income."

"Papa! You must not accept money from him!" Juliana, horrified, tried to remonstrate. In all conscience, she could not have Ranceford out of pocket over this affair, no matter how odious he might be.

"Oh, can I not!" her father carolled. "A magnificent settlement indeed. More than I had hoped. Oh, and there's a stipulation that a deal of the first payment is to go for your wedding clothes. You may call in a mantua maker at once—and a milliner—a furrier—whatever you choose." He pottered happily towards the door. "A new coat for myself—Weston, of course—some shirts and a pair of those new pantaloons..." His voice faded as he went down the hall. "...And a new velvet dressing-gown..."

A frantic message went forth to the masked man, by way of One-eye Willyum, who frequented the Beveridge House kitchen. The reply cast her in some doubt, for he advised her to accept, saying Ranceford could afford it.

It did not seem honourable somehow, but she desperately needed a few gowns and a new pelisse with matching bonnet. She kept her purchases to a minimum, selecting practical garments and adding only a riding habit in case her Corsair came for her on the black horse as he promised—or at least implied. Such an abduction at the altar would certainly add spice to the ceremony, and they might have to ride hard and far if the jilted lord pursued them. But surely he would not. It would be beneath the dignity of such a high-in-the-instep gentleman.

She wished she could discuss the matter with her masked man in person, but during the entire three weeks she saw nothing of him. Her faith was only sustained by the periodic notes sent via One-eye Willyum and Emily Jane, assuring her of the evolving of his plans and that all was in train. Her own plans consisted of packing up the few treasured belongings with which she could not part, for Emily Jane to send on when she knew where she'd be.

A week before the scheduled ceremony, a huge box arrived, containing a gift from her godmama, a gown copied from an illustration in the French *Journal des Dames* of a wedding ensemble in blue and white with a matching veil. Juliana opened the box and, folding back the silver paper, gazed in awe at her first fairy-tale toilette. Her hands trembled as she lifted the gown and shook out shimmering folds of palest blue point lace over a white satin underdress with silver foil trim at the hem.

The high-waisted skirt bore no fewer than three deep lace flounces, each caught up in alternating festooned tiers by bouquets of white satin roses and silver rib-bon knots. A rouleau of satin lozenges caught by more silver knots and rosebuds edged the very low neckline of the smallest possible corsage. The tiny sleeves were puffs of the lace over satin, decorated top and bot-tom with the same rouleaux of satin lozenges, silver knots, and rosebuds. With it was to be worn a long scarf of white veiling, edged with the pale blue lace, and gathered at the centre, where it was attached to a garland of white satin roses for her headdress. The ends of the scarf fell in cascades, looped over the el-bows, and trailed to the floor on both sides.

There was more. In the bottom of the box Juliana found white satin slippers, long white kid gloves, and a matching lace-and-satin reticule in the form of a huge white rose to be hung from her wrist on loops of satin ribbon ending in bows and rosebuds.

For a long time, she sat on the edge of her bed, now and then touching the delicate fabrics. What would dearest Godmama Amelia think when all this beauty was carried off on a great prancing black horse? She could only hope to be forgiven some day, for wear this gown she would. She'd never have another chance.

Emily Jane was ecstatic over the gown. "Blue lace!" she exclaimed, delighted. "You know the saying. 'A bride 'oo wears blue will always be true.' Oh, Miss Julie, surely it's an omen."

Emily Jane was at her most exasperating during this period. Her own nuptuals were scheduled to take place as soon as Juliana was wed—to whichever man. Full of smirks and giggles, she cheerfully spouted superstitions and proverbs. She warned Juliana never to let anyone sweep beneath her feet and even ceased cleaning her bedchamber, lest the marriage be postponed. A series of overcast days sent her into gloom for fear it might rain on the wedding day. She reminded Juliana that for a fortunate marriage, she must stand with her feet going the same direction as the cracks in the floor and must take her first step after the ceremony with her right foot. And on their commencing the journey to Gretna Green, she advised her to stop and pick up a rock at the first crossroad, to carry in her pocket for luck until she was securely wed. Emily Jane had to be forcibly discouraged from filling Juliana's room with offerings of apples, bananas, tomatoes and catnip, all guaranteed to ensure a fruitful marriage. Frequently she succumbed to a painful bout of hiccoughs in her efforts to keep from giggling. It almost seemed, Juliana thought, that Emily Jane was concealing a greater secret than that of her mistress's elopement.

THE MARQUIS OF RANCEFORD, meanwhile, had found Lady Clara's new meek and subservient role harder to bear than her jovial chatter.

Her obsequious manners and constant concern for his every need quite got in amongst him, and he hoped to rouse her back to normal with his cataclysmic news. He therefore took the bull by the horns, figuratively speaking, and informed his sister-in-law of his intention to wed the daughter of Sir Agramont Beveridge in a few weeks' time, awaiting only the posting of the banns on the three successive Sundays.

Lady Clara took it amazingly well, even to the point of accepting the blame.

"It is all my fault!" she wailed. "I put the Beveridge chit into your head and only see what has come of it." She discovered a bright spot and rallied. "How fortunate that Lady Catherine has just been brought down by the measles and need not feel obliged to attend the service. Indeed, I have only this morning received a most unpleasant note from her regarding my allowing the girls to give dear Hubert the contagious disease. How was I to know she had not had them and would catch them from him?"

Other bright spots appeared, but not those Lady Clara feared. The girls, Augusta, Rosamund and Ophelia, would be quite free from the measles by then, and she warded off further complexion problems with every beauty aid mentioned in *La Belle Assemblée*, in the hope they would develop no others, for they were to take part in the ceremony as attendants. Their freckles were attacked by night with Roman balsam, a paste of barley flour, honey, and bitter almonds. By day, the girls languished on couches for hours beneath layers of crushed strawberries, alternating with washes of *Eau de Ninon* and distilled water of pineapples. Ethelinda and Mirabella, thankfully too young for such problems, were scheduled to scatter flowers.

"I wonder, Ranceford—" Clara tapped a fingertip against her protruding front teeth "—under the circumstances, if it would not be polite to invite young Hubert to be ring bearer?"

"No," said Rance flatly. "And I think you'd best consult with Amelia Robertshaw. She is the girl's godmother, and no doubt will have something to say about the plans."

Lady Clara nodded briskly. "So much easier to deal with than Lady Catherine. Do you know, I never actually did like the creature, but she was so suitable."

"She didn't suit me, and Miss Beveridge does."

His sister-in-law waxed philosophical. "Perhaps you know best. Lady Catherine, unfortunately, has a somewhat forceful character. This little nobody will no doubt make you a quiet, biddable wife and mother for your children."

Rance looked at her. He didn't answer.

AFTER WHAT SEEMED a year to Juliana, the fateful day arrived. All plans were complete. The Conkleys and Emily Jane had decorated the tiny chapel at the back of the house with flowers from the garden. Amelia

Robertshaw, with Sir Agramont and Lord Rance-ford, had contrived the entire affair. During their conferences, Juliana hid in her bedchamber from the marquis, for she could not face him after spending his money on garments to wear in company with another man. The meetings transpired with what sounded to be an excessive amount of enjoyment. *Let them be happy while they can,* she thought, feeling left out in spite of what she meant to do.

In the secrecy of her room, she even tried to don the riding habit beneath her wedding gown, with disas-trous results. The bulk of the heavier garment split the seams of the bodice, and she and Emily Jane spent the last few minutes of her dressing time frantically mak-ing repairs while the abigail giggled until Juliana came near to throttling her.

The floor clock in the front hall struck ten, the hour for the Beveridge household to assemble in the tiny chapel. It was to be a simple, private ceremony as was currently in vogue, with only her godparents and Ranceford's family in attendance.

Waiting in the close chapel, Juliana felt near swooning like Adorinda from anticipation and the overpowering scent of the flowers, even though the double doors stood open to the courtyard. The Mar-quis of Ranceford and his family had not yet ap-peared, but the Robertshaws had arrived in their elegant carriage, prepared to stand as witnesses.

Juliana wore Lady Robertshaw's exquisite wedding gown, adding only her mother's pearl necklet and earrings. There were tears in her godmother's eyes when she hugged her in greeting and Juliana, wrought up as never before, nearly wept as well.

Searching for relief from her taut nerves, she fixed her attention on Lady Robertshaw's spectacular French bonnet, a concoction of capucine velvet, levantine, and blond lace ruffles, topped with a high plume of *jonquille* ostrich feathers. A few minutes were safely passed in compliments. And still, no sign of the marquis—or her masked Corsair.

The Robertshaws had brought their two eldest daughters, and the girls were unaccountably subject to fits of titters interspersed with nudges and whispers. Juliana considered their manners most inappropriate, since this was a solemn occasion and for her, at least, one fraught with terror and suspense.

Would her Corsair come as he promised? Had his plans gone awry? Suppose Ranceford came first and she was wed before the masked man could save her?

Then hoofbeats sounded without the garden wall and Juliana's pulse galloped in time to their beat. One horse only—could it be? Yes! In moments, the great black horse cantered across the courtyard and right through the open chapel doors. The Robertshaws screamed and their daughters shouted with delight, causing Pacha to dance among the pews, scattering prayer-books and knee pillows, before his caped rider got him under control.

Her Corsair grinned down at her, the eyes behind his mask warm with appreciation. "My," he said. "Are we not fine!"

Juliana flew to his side. "Oh, take me away, quickly!"

"Use that pew for a mounting block, my Adorinda," he ordered, kicking his near foot from the stirrup.

She needed no more. Throwing the trailing ends of her veiling about her shoulders, out of her way, she scrambled onto the pew seat and placed her foot in the empty stirrup. He swung her up side-saddle before him with a shattering unconcern for her lace and roses. She found she didn't care. His strong arm circled her waist as Pacha reared and spun, his hooves clattering on the ancient stone floor as he trotted out of the chapel, across the courtyard, and into the street beyond.

Juliana twisted so she could put her arms about the masked man's neck, and she tried to kiss his chin, but Pacha's trot was not his best gait.

"You came!" she exclaimed. "And just in time!"

"Could you doubt me?" He drew her close and his breath stirred the curls by her ear.

She sighed happily. "Where are we going?"

"To be married, my love, if that is your pleasure."

"Oh, yes, please—but not all the way to Gretna Green aboard this horse, I hope, for I'm finding this method of travel exceedingly uncomfortable."

He laughed, a joyous triumphant shout, and had to pull Pacha back down to all four feet. He slowed the horse to a sedate walk, a pace which made Juliana more uncomfortable than the trot.

"Should we not make speed?" she asked nervously. "Ranceford may pursue us."

The Corsair chuckled. "Have no fear. His lordship will not stop our marriage. We ride only to the nearest church, my love. We'll then leave Pacha with Willyum and go on to Italy."

"Italy!"

"You don't care for Italy? France, then, if you prefer. You know," he added conversationally, "I was not at all sure this beast would carry double—"

"What!"

"—So I practised with Willyum."

Juliana giggled like Emily Jane. "I never thought to arrive at my wedding on horseback."

"Nor did I." He nuzzled his nose into the curls by her ear. "But I felt it to be a fitting start for our life of adventure. Ah, here we are. Hanover Square."

As they rode up to St. George's, One-eye Willyum appeared as from nowhere and took a firm hold on Pacha's bridle while the masked man slid Juliana from the horse's back, landing her safely on the cobbles before he joined her. Unclasping his cape, he doffed it with a swirl of black and crimson. Juliana hadn't noticed, in all the excitement, that under his cloak he wore the impeccable formal attire of a gentleman. He handed the cape to Emily Jane. Where had she come from? Then Juliana spied the Conkleys and realized John Coachman must have driven them all over at a

gallop. So that was why the masked man had walked
Pacha so slowly!

He led her up the steps to the open church doors.
People filled the pews inside. Musicians struck up an
air at that moment, and Juliana clutched his hand.
"We cannot go in! There is already a formal affair in
progress." She hung back. He tried to urge her on, but
she remained glued to the spot. "We shall have to
wait. Is there not a side door?"

Beneath the black mask, his teeth flashed in a grin.
"It is all right. The rector has promised to give us
whatever time we need."

"But we cannot go in wearing that mask! Do take
it off."

He hesitated, as though uncertain. "Suppose—
suppose you find my face displeasing?"

"Nonsense. It is *you* I care for, not some classic
Greek god."

His lips quirked in amusement. "Like your Marquis of Ranceford."

"Oh, him. I grant you he is exceedingly handsome,
but he is not my Corsair."

His smile went a trifle awry. "My love, I fear he is."
He undid the strip of silk and waited, silent, for her
reaction. It was not slow in coming.

"Ranceford!" She pushed him away, wrathful.
"You have tricked me! *You* cannot be my masked
man! Oh, how could you have deceived me so?"

"Believe me, it is I. Has been all along."

"Ranceford! You truly are *Ranceford!*"

They remained standing in the doorway, oblivious to the stares of the gaily dressed people within. He tried to take her hands, but she thrust them behind her.

"Please, Juliana. How could I reveal myself to you when you were so patently prepared to hate me? You would not have given me a chance. I had to win you, any way I could."

He was right. Juliana backed a step, shaking her head, trying to accept the man standing before her as her beloved Gothic hero.

He put out a tentative hand. "I was afraid you would not accept my offer."

"I—I didn't. My father did."

"Oh, but you did. At the foot of your garden, three weeks ago, you granted my every dream."

"But that wasn't you!" Her sensation of shock lingered. "That was my masked man!"

"Shall I put it back on? I'll wear it forever if it means you will be my Adorinda and live with me in a hovel. Juliana—say you will instead be my marchioness, for I cannot live out my role without you as my heroine."

She still felt dazed. "If you are Ranceford . . . then all this is for us?"

"It is the fault of my sister-in-law, Lady Clara," he apologized. "She feels no marriage is legal unless performed with great pomp in St. George's. And I fear you will have to face a sad crush at our reception at Ranceford House. Clara has been in her element."

"Lady Clara! I had quite forgot her! Ranceford, I could not live in a house managed by another woman."

She seemed to be melting. He seized the advantage. "Clara has removed to the Dower House, and taken the girls with her. We shall be quite alone. Your father can stay where he is. Currently, however, he is awaiting us at the altar."

As were the rest of the company. Juliana, peering inside, saw far up in the front the *jonquille* plumes of Lady Robertshaw's new hat. She patted wildly at her hair, disarranged by their ride. "I cannot go in there! I must look a fright!"

Emily Jane was at her side at once, smoothing the veiling and dusting her skirts, all the while clucking like a hen over her chick.

Rance shook his head and gently pushed the abigail away. He bent to kiss the tip of Juliana's nose.

"Now do stop carrying on like a distracted Gothic heroine," he murmured, his voice low and throbbing—this time, low for her ears only and throbbing from his underlying happiness. "You love me, whoever I am, and you know it."

He swept her into his arms and proved, beyond a shadow of a doubt, that a staid and respectable marquis could be as romantic as any Corsair conceived by a poet.

Juliana responded with all her being, lost in the wonder of giving herself totally to the only man in the world. Safe in his warm embrace, she snuggled against his broad chest.

"Oh, yes," she whispered. "Now I do know. You *are* my masked man."

His deep, satisfied chuckle rumbled beneath her cheek. He turned her towards the aisle. "Come, my Adorinda, our novel has reached its happy beginning."

She tried to remember in which direction to point her feet....

Summer Reading At Its Best

In July, Harlequin and Silhouette bring readers the Big Summer Read Program. Heat up your summer with these four exciting new novels by top Harlequin and Silhouette authors.

SOMEWHERE IN TIME by Barbara Bretton
YESTERDAY COMES TOMORROW by Rebecca Flanders
A DAY IN APRIL by Mary Lynn Baxter
LOVE CHILD by Patricia Coughlin

From time travel to fame and fortune, this program offers something for everyone.

Available at your favorite retail outlet.

BSR

Harlequin®

JANELLE TAYLOR

Valley of Fire

HARLEQUIN IS PROUD TO PRESENT *VALLEY OF FIRE* BY JANELLE TAYLOR—AUTHOR OF TWENTY-TWO BOOKS, INCLUDING SIX *NEW YORK TIMES* BESTSELLERS

VALLEY OF FIRE—the warm and passionate story of Kathy Alexander, a famous romance author, and Steven Winngate, entrepreneur and owner of the magazine that intended to expose the real Kathy "Brandy" Alexander to her fans.

Don't miss VALLEY OF FIRE, available in May.

Take 4 bestselling love stories FREE

Plus get a FREE surprise gift!

OVER THE YEARS, TELEVISION HAS BROUGHT
THE LIVES AND LOVES OF MANY CHARACTERS INTO
YOUR HOMES. NOW HARLEQUIN INTRODUCES YOU
TO THE TOWN AND PEOPLE OF

One small town—twelve terrific love stories.

GREAT READING...GREAT SAVINGS...AND A FABULOUS
FREE GIFT!

Each book set in Tyler is a self-contained love story; together, the
twelve novels stitch the fabric of the community.

By collecting proofs-of-purchase found in each Tyler book, you can
receive a fabulous gift, ABSOLUTELY FREE! And use our special
Tyler coupons to save on your next TYLER book purchase.

Join us for the fourth TYLER book,
MONKEY WRENCH by Nancy Martin.

*Can elderly Rose Atkins successfully bring a new love into
granddaughter Susannah's life?*

If you missed *Whirlwind* (March), *Bright Hopes* (April) or *Wisconsin Wedding* (May), and would
like to order them, send your name, address, zip or postal code, along with a check or money
order for $3.99 (please do not send cash), plus 75¢ postage and handling ($1.00 in Canada),
for each book ordered, payable to Harlequin Reader Service to:

In the U.S.

3010 Walden Avenue
P.O. Box 1325
Buffalo, NY 14269-1325

In Canada

P.O. Box 609
Fort Erie, Ontario
L2A 5X3

Please specify book title(s) with your order.
Canadian residents add applicable federal and provincial taxes.

TYLER-4

FREE GIFT OFFER

To receive your free gift, send us the specified number of proofs-of-purchase from any specially marked Free Gift Offer Harlequin or Silhouette book with the Free Gift Certificate properly completed, plus a check or money order (do not send cash) to cover postage and handling payable to Harlequin/Silhouette Free Gift Promotion Offer. We will send you the specified gift.

FREE GIFT CERTIFICATE

ITEM	A. GOLD TONE EARRINGS	B. GOLD TONE BRACELET	C. GOLD TONE NECKLACE
# of proofs-of-purchase required	3	6	9
Postage and Handling	$1.75	$2.25	$2.75
Check one	☐	☐	☐

Name: _____

Address: _____

City: _____ State: _____ Zip Code: _____

Mail this certificate, specified number of proofs-of-purchase and a check or money order for postage and handling to: HARLEQUIN/SILHOUETTE FREE GIFT OFFER 1992, P.O. Box 9057, Buffalo, NY 14269-9057. Requests must be received by July 31, 1992.

PLUS—Every time you submit a completed certificate with the correct number of proofs-of-purchase, you are automatically entered in our MILLION DOLLAR SWEEPSTAKES! No purchase or obligation necessary to enter. See below for alternate means of entry and how to obtain complete sweepstakes rules.

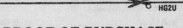

HG2U

ONE PROOF-OF-PURCHASE
To collect your fabulous FREE GIFT you must include the necessary FREE GIFT proofs-of-purchase with a properly completed offer certificate.

(See inside back cover for offer details)